To Gene —
keeps the Ioxe Writers Group ... e

Nolan C. Lewis 6/3/04

MAULED

BY NOLAN LEWIS

PublishAmerica

Baltimore

ISBN: 1-4137-1215-0
PUBLISHED BY PUBLISHAMERICA, LLLP
www.publishamerica.com
Baltimore

Printed in the United States of America

Dedicated to Mickey, who has suffered through this with me, whilst I stare at the wall or blindly out the window for hours on end.

CHAPTER ONE

It finally registered. The discordant clamor wasn't inside my head. I had discovered a long time ago that a phone is too delicate to live long on the bedside table, within easy reach, when it has no better sense than to waken me from a sound sleep. A one-eyed peek and I knew it was either too early or the weather was too lousy for anyone important to be on the other end.

With my usual quick reaction in times of stress, I yanked the pillow down over my head and did my damnedest to go back to sleep. The elbow between my shoulder blades after the fourth ring reminded me that some others are not quite so quick. So I rolled over and pulled the other pillow from under the rust-colored hair that adorned it and jammed it down on top.

I knew I wasn't getting away with it when I felt the bed rebound and heard the thud of angry steps around the foot. I wasn't sure of the winner… If the caller gave up or Sherry picked up in time, but the jangling stopped… Momentarily that is.

The loud clatter of the base of the phone bouncing off the table, across the floor, and into the metal of the bed frame was not promising, so I lifted a corner of the pillow for a peek. Immediately in front of my nose was a curly, rust-colored triangle, framed by well-rounded hips. A little wider view revealed the lushly upholstered body leaning very unselfconsciously over the edge of the bed, with the phone handset dangling by its cord from two fingers as if she were holding a snake. The fire darting from the two green eyes in the pert face above dared me to continue to ignore the interloper.

With my usual lightning reflexes I made a two-finger grab at the soft mat in front of my nose, and ended up with a handful of that softest part of the female anatomy when Sherry took a quick step backward and in the process leaned down over the bed. I also got the phone, none to gently, along side my head. It lay there on the bed beside my ear, still spewing its unintelligible metallic noises.

She spoke the first words of the day when she said, "Answer the dumb phone," and crawled across me to get back under the covers and out of the morning's dank chill.

I could recognize the voice before I got the phone close to my ear… Actually, I didn't want it too close, my eardrum would never handle it. "God damn you! Don't you lay the phone down and go back to sleep!"

It was Charley, my editor, or at least he called himself that when he wanted something from me. Charley Shehan, editor of the paper across the Columbia, who I sort of worked for, somewhere between a correspondent and stringer. He usually called me when he figured the story wasn't worth sending a man on, or it was the weekend and he would have to pay overtime to somebody to get it covered. This being Saturday morning, it was easy to figure it was the latter. After my third, "Hello Charley," the phone finally quit spitting long enough for me to get a word in. "Morning Charley, what the hell got you all stirred up this early on Saturday morn…"

"What do you mean 'early'? It's after nine. You're gonna sleep your whole damn life away."

Obviously he lived by a different clock. "OK Charley, you got me awake now anyway, what you got?"

"Some guy over there got croaked last night. I don't have anybody on today."

"Yeah… How come you didn't just call the sheriff's office?" I knew he didn't have a paper short of Monday. "What was it this time anyway, knife or gun?" The local rednecks are predictable. If someone gets a knife stuck in them, the cops look toward a fisherman or fish cannery worker; if it's a gun they favor a logger.

"No… This guy got done in bed. Not sure if it was a hammer or an axe. Pretty messy I hear. Take your camera, we might use some art."

"OK Charley, I'm too awake now to get any more sleep anyway. I'll see what I can find out."

"Keep me posted. Don't wait until deadline and dump a bunch of shit last minute."

"OK Charley, I'll keep you posted. Bye."

Remembering the feel of a few minutes ago, I rolled over and snuggled against the warm body next to mine and ran a hand under the arm to explore. She is, in at least one man's opinion, a great example of how to distribute a hundred thirty-five pounds on a five foot four female frame, in order to attain the most tantalizing package possible. Sherry said, "Damn, didn't you take care of that last night? Why don't you go put a pot on like a good boy," as she turned firmly onto her stomach.

Knowing full well I was going to get nowhere, I gave up and rolled out into the cold air. First things first, a brief stop in the can. I couldn't resist a look in the cloudy mirror as I washed my hands—I'm definitely not improving with age.

Blue eyes, rimmed by red from last night's debauchery, in an elongated face that was much in need of a shave, peering out from between what I liked to call laugh lines. I never could figure why a beard should be so black in just twenty-four hours, when hair on top of the head was dishwater brown.

I shivered across the living room/office/kitchen to the sink to do as requested. A glance out the mildew-rimmed window and I knew why it was still half dark. Just the usual coastal weather for November: Wind and rain.

As I was pouring the water I heard, "What did he want?" from the bedroom.

I astutely answered, "Huh?"

"That was Charley Shehan wasn't it? What did he want? What's going on?"

"Oh… Somebody got bumped off last night or something. Can't be too much or he woulda sent one of his own men. I'll make a couple of phone calls after a while and put something together. He doesn't have a deadline 'till Monday anyhow and will probably send one of his reporters over Monday to keep his costs down."

I had moved across the room during this discourse, until I was slouching in the bedroom door. Not a door really, actually the whole wall was a temporary partition someone a long time ago strung across the end of the previous room, an L-shape formed when one corner of the original square room was walled off to create a bath. The other end of the room held a small table and a couple of chairs *a la* dining room, and a two-burner electric range, a small sink that was at present heaped with a day or two worth of dirty dishes, and a small 1950s refrigerator, they called a kitchenette.

The door hole into the bedroom was tall enough to accommodate my six foot two, before they installed the rod across for the curtain that would be the door, if the door still existed. "Furnished," with hand me down garage-sale furniture of cracked vinyl and mismatched chairs, it is typical of half of the old motel units converted to living quarters here at the beach. Their single redeeming feature is that the rents are cheap. It is the only thing most of the people employed in the tourist industry, and freelance writers with infrequent sales and minuscule royalty checks, can afford.

Sufficiently interested now to roll over, Sherry asked, "He say who?" At my negative grunt, she asked, "Knife or gun this time?"

"No… Someone did the Lizzie Borden on this guy."

This caught her attention enough that she sat up in bed, exposing my favorite playthings. She said, "My god, Frank. You just gonna stand there in the door looking obscene all day? What the hell you do with the robe I bought you?"

"It's around someplace. Trouble is it's never where I need it…besides, look who's talking. How about I hop back in bed while

8

the coffee cooks?"

"You mean we got somebody running around killing people with an axe?"

"Not people. Person."

"God's sake. Get some clothes on and make some calls. I might luck out and get this one as a PD." Sherry with clothes on is a lawyer. The gold leaf on her window says "S. J. Thompkins, Attorney at Law." I kid her about how she uses the initials so the prospects won't find out her sex, because a lot of the rednecks around the town wouldn't believe a woman capable of doing the job. With less than ten thousand souls in the whole county, she can't afford to let any get away. An occasional appointment as Public Defender helps to keep her solvent. Most weekends she slums. That is, she spends them here with me.

"All right… It seems a terrible waste, but I'll get my pants on. Calling is gonna have to wait 'til I get some coffee. My brain won't work without."

"Ok! Bring! You got anything out there to eat? Anything you won't have to scrape the whiskers off anyway?"

I went through to the sink and rinsed the booze out of last night's mugs and filled them with coffee. Before carrying them to the other room I made a halfhearted check of the one possible cupboard and the refrigerator. "Nothing but half a loaf of rye… I could make some toast?"

"Hate it. It probably has bugs and I can't tell them from the seeds," she said with a disgusted look upon her face.

After a few sips of the hot black liquid, I suggested, "How you expect me to concentrate with those two staring at me? Maybe I could slip back in bed and nibble on the pink part, just a little bit."

"Damn old letch."

"What you mean 'old'? I'm only twenty-nine."

"Yeah. You and Jack Benny. You'll never see thirty again. Bet you got kids somewhere, damn near as old as me." This last was delivered as I watched the delicious curves disappear into the bathroom. Truth is, I'm thirty-seven, making me eight years her senior. Twenty-nine came hard for her when it struck so unexpectedly a couple months back.

After refilling my cup I picked up the phone and sitting cross-legged on the bed I dialed the home number of Bernie Holmes, police chief and the only member of the local three-man police force who would be apt to give me as much as the correct time. Actually, he is chief of police at Long Beach, three miles up the highway. Oceanside is so small they don't have their own and contract it out. His wife picked up on the second ring and after a cheery hello, she informed me Bernie wasn't home and had been working most of the night. I got lucky on the next call as Bernie answered the phone, but I could tell by his guarded answer when I told him who it was that he wasn't alone. I asked, "Got lots of help there this morning?"

"Yeah."

"County?"

"Yeah."

"State."

"Yeah."

"Bet you're having a barrel of laughs. Heard we lost another good citizen last night. What's the victim's name?"

"I'm not sure I should..."

"Aw, come on Bernie. You know I can't do anything with it until Monday. Long before that the County Attorney will put it out on the wires and the TV guys will be all over you. At least you know I'll spell your name right."

"OK, Ankus." He knows that gripes my ass. Somebody with a sense of humor named me Ankus Franklin Thomas Hill. I prefer Tom; some, including Sherry on occasion, call me Frank, but no one ever calls me Ankus unless they are looking for a fight or know they have me where I can't do anything about it. "The guy's name was Suolo Kaakani." At my request he spelled it for me and then remarked, "Good Finn name."

"Thanks Bernie. Where did he live?"

"I already gave you more than I should."

"Come on Bernie. You know these Oceanside phone books just list the town. No addresses."

"Shit, you want me to write it for you too? OK, he lived in an old trailer about quarter mile northeast of Oceanside, off 101 on the right."

10

"Thanks Bernie. I'm going to dig around a little. I find out anything I think might help you, I'll give it to you personal."

"Better not go out there digging around... Least you do, don't mention my name."

"Any suspects yet?"

"You got all you're gonna get... More than I should've given you anyway."

"Right. Thanks Bernie. I won't forget."

"Bernie Holmes?" At my nod she asked, "What did you find out?"

"Not much. He had an office full of county and state cops so he wasn't saying much. The scene of the dastardly deed is only about half a mile from here at the edge of town," I said as I began pulling on my clothes. Sherry started doing likewise.

CHAPTER TWO

Fortified by a pot of coffee, I slung my camera bag over my shoulder and started toward my car. Sherry said, "Let's take mine. I'll drive you."

"Who said you were invited?"

"We take mine. At least you know you will get there and back. That old heap of yours is just looking for a quiet place to die with dignity."

"Shit! I need a chiropractor every time I do this," I said as I folded my legs and ducked my head to get into her Z car. She tooled it expertly out of the lot and headed out the highway. At the light, the town only has one, we had to wait while two four-wheel pickups, jacked up to where we could have driven under them, squealed around the corner. The gun racks in both back windows were full. The second one had a rack on the back of the truck and there were two men with long guns, either rifles or shotguns, standing up in the rear and leaning over the cab, in spite of the weather.

I gripe about riding with Sherry, but have to admit she drives pretty good. I like to sit and watch… Or maybe I just like to sit and watch her move whether she is driving or not. She does nice things to her coast formal outfit… Blue jeans and hooded sweat shirt. I keep thinking, *some day I'll have to consider maybe making this arrangement more permanent*, but then I rethink, *why ruin a great friendship?*

The place was easy to spot. Half a dozen blocks through town and we wound our way up over the hill. Just as we started down the other side, she began to brake. The trees along the roadside for a couple hundred feet were decorated with yellow ribbons, with "Police Lines Do Not Cross" in three inch letters down the length.

"Don't stop. Ease on by and turn around and park in that drive across the street." She gave me one of her looks, but did as I asked, without comment.

As we passed I could see two reserve deputies standing in the driveway that led to an old single wide trailer, once white, but now mostly green with algae, parked a hundred feet or so back in the alder trees. It was plainly visible because the trees were all bare, having long since deposited their yearly quota of leaves on top of last year's and probably several years' before, on the roof of the trailer as well as the ground around it.

As Sherry slipped into the drive I got my camera ready. I was half out of the car when I remembered… We had been out on the jetty by the lighthouse yesterday and the camera was loaded with color. If I shot that it would take me a week to get the film processed around here.

While it rewound itself I fumbled in the bag and dug out a roll of Tri-X and when it stopped grinding, slipped it in. The two reserve deputies across the highway were standing on opposite sides of the drive, raincoats tucked behind holsters, practicing their quick draw on each other, totally unaware of us. Just for fun I squeezed off a couple shots. With the lens zoomed out they framed nicely. Never can tell when a picture like that will come in handy.

I walked casually across the road and said, "Hi fellows." Before either one could come out with a stance that would be hard to get him off, I added, "They told me down at the cop shop you were out here. Pretty messy huh?"

One of the deputies said, "I don't know… We're not supposed…"

The other asked, "Say, aren't you that writer guy… Lives down there in the old Blue Gull Motel."

"Pretty sharp. Just here to get something for the paper. Picture of the trailer I guess. I'm sure they already moved the stiff." At the second deputy's nod I said, "That's OK… I've seen enough bodies anyway. They said he got done with an axe. That place must be a real mess?"

The friendly deputy said, "Splitting maul actually, and it really wasn't that bad. Not nearly as much blood as you would expect."

The other looked a warning at him, so I took another tack. I said, "How about you fellows moving down towards the trailer a few feet and stand on each side of the road. The newspaper is going to want something so I'll get a couple shots of you guys guarding the place."

"Now one on each side of the road. I need just a couple steps," as I ducked under the ribbon. The less friendly man raised his hand to protest and I said, "Yes, hold that," and I shot one, then zoomed the lens out where I framed the trailer neatly by itself between the two men and squeezed off a couple more. I said, "Let Sherry get your names so we're sure to spell them right."

While they were spelling them for her I said, "Let's see, the guy's name was…" flipping through my notebook I made a halfway try at the name and asked, "Apparently not married from the looks of the place?"

With a grin, the helpful deputy said, "Good Finnish name. I have trouble with it too. Yeah he was married… Or maybe just shacked up… Old lady works down at the Safehaven Tavern, down there on the docks."

The second deputy added, "Married… I stopped her once and ran her license. Real looker…Melannie I think." Then he flipped out his notebook. "Yeah Melannie, with two Ns. Don't think she always remembers she's married though. Wonder if she had him insured?"

"That ugly Finn? There would sure have to be some reason why a good-looking piece like that would put up with him. S'cuse me ma'am."

"Either one of you know anything about the guy they are holding for this?"

"You mean the kid? Don't think they caught up with him yet. Jimmy

Beasley? Yeah, we know him. Not too smart. Been in the South Bend Hilton a couple times. Penny ante stuff like shoplifting. Dumb things like cheap fishing tackle. He does odd jobs around."

"How they come up with his name? Doesn't sound like somebody you'd expect to do something like this."

"Phone call I guess. I hear it was anonymous."

The recalcitrant cut in with, "We're really not supposed to talk too much. The Sarge said…"

"I got most of it from the cop shop before we came down… I'll never tell. How about another picture of you guys standing behind the ribbon? Yeah, put your hand on your gun. You got the names straight Sherry? Always got to get the names right."

.   Back in the car I said, "You listen real good… Sure you got those names right?" Then ducked the notebook she launched across the car.

"You'd make a good lawyer. You jerked those guys around pretty good. You know it's really not legal to lie to the cops like that though." Then she asked, "What's a splitting maul? Sounds nasty."

"Sort of like a fat axe, or maybe a wedge on a handle. Probably weighs about eight or nine pounds. Good for splitting wood. You can usually split a block of wood with one swing… Or maybe even a Finn head I guess, with a couple swings."

"That's more than I really wanted to know. It sounds even nastier than an ax. Where to next?"

"Need to check out that wife, but it's still to early to hit the tavern. I'll let you buy breakfast. Even let you pick the place."

"We could go up to Long Beach and hit the bakery. You can hear about anything going on in the whole south county. These local people don't need a newspaper, long as they have the bakery. Sorry if that hurts your feelings. We might hear something useful though."

"Damn… Make a reporter out of you yet."

"And we could also get something to eat before I get as skinny as you."

In the short drive, the rains began again in earnest. I've never been sure, is the weather that different three or four miles away, or have the

15

rains moved in at both places? As is normal in the winter the street was mostly empty, except for a few cars in front of the bakery. So we dripped our way in, and found seats after snagging a large cinnamon roll and a coffee each at the counter.

I've only lived in the area for about four years, so I am still a tourist as far as the old timers are concerned. They totally ignore me. This is sometimes helpful because the invisibility makes eavesdropping easier. Sherry is from an old peninsula family so she is in a different category, even though she did leave for several years and had just recently returned. She was greeted by most as if she were family but they tended to look across me without even acknowledging I was present.

The locals always congregate at the tables in the front windows, where they can observe the "pukers." This is the colloquial name for the tourists, a reference to how they spend a good share of their time at the rail when out on the charter boats. The natives usually sit and take turns making snide comments about those passing by on the sidewalk as they hash over the latest gossip.

This was a day off for the few tourists willing to brave the weather, and all of the talk was about the murder of the night before. All of the lurid details, considered secret by the police, were rehashed every time a newcomer joined the group, and most had a few of their own to add. They knew the supposed secret name of the kid, the prime suspect. Opinion was divided on his guilt, and if he even had enough smarts to do the deed.

Everyone also seemed to be aware of the manhunt going on. Not by the police, but by a bunch of the local ne'er-do-wells in their four-wheel drive trucks. A good share were of the opinion he should be fair game. "Wouldn't be hiding out if he wasn't guilty." The odds were about even on whether they would be able to find him. It was about sixty-forty they wouldn't bring him in alive if they did. No one appeared to be very much disturbed with the idea.

One of the later arrivals was a retired tavern owner, who still claimed to be privy to some of the inside knowledge of the lower elements. She said in her gravel voice, "They need to look into that wife of his. She ain't no better than she needs to be. Her and the owner of that joint.

You can bet she does more for him than tend his bar. Only reason she could have married that ugly Finn was if he had a lot of insurance."

All joined in speculating on this relationship. Most knew little personally, but no one was averse to adding their opinion. Mostly it added little fact to what we already knew. Then the old gal dropped in another zinger. "I wouldn't be surprised if he wasn't the anonymous tipster that set the cops on the kid." I couldn't for the life of me understand how they all knew more of what was going on than I had been able to pry out of the cops.

"Suppose we should go check that joint out," Sherry asked.

"Gonna have to eventually, but I'm not sure I could handle it in the daylight. You ever been in there?"

"Not sober. Stumbled in there a couple of times when a bunch of us were out partying."

As we headed out to the car I said, "Suppose it wouldn't hurt to drop by that joint for a few minutes. See what the day shift is talking about. Really won't get anything solid until the night crowd gets loosened a bit." I settled back and listened to the swish of the tires on the wet pavement and the monotonous click of the wipers.

As Sherry pulled into the parking across from the Safehaven it was hard to tell if there was anyone inside or not. It answered one question, it was raining down here now also. The small, smoked-up windows of the tavern passed the light of the red beer sign inside, but little else. The once red building had lost half its paint to the unkind coast environment and the rain made it look uninviting and ominous even in the daylight.

Sherry said, "Never noticed in the dark, but this place actually hangs out over the water."

"Yeah. I've heard stories about trap doors and Shanghaiing in the old days. Not a good place to get someone pissed at you. They throw you out the back door it would be a cold swim. Whoever named the joint had some kind of sense of humor."

The inside was no cleaner than the windows. The bar ran down the left side of the room. It began some fifteen feet from the door, open at both ends, with a separation in its center. The few patrons were sitting in a group at the rear half. The several tables were vacant, but one of the two pool tables had the remains of a pool game. The whole place smelled strongly of fish, stale beer, dirty ashtrays, unwashed bodies, and really badly of urine.

The first two things were explained by the two people leaning across their stool backs, as if in a deep conversation with the rest of the group. One was a tall skinny guy and the other was just plain big. Both had pool cues in their hands and both were dressed in rain gear and rubber boots, identifying them as working in the fish cannery down the dock.

At the sound of the door closing behind us, all present turned to look and conversation stopped. We took seats at a table, as close to the group as we could without being too obvious. Trying for smart, I said, "Suppose those two guys are playing pool, or you think they are boy scouts… You know, always prepared."

Sherry gave me a pained look and returned, "You are getting old. That one is not a guy." Catching the direction of my look she added, "No not the skinny one. The big one."

"Maybe we should challenge the table. Maybe it would get a conversation started."

"Better than challenging her to arm wrestle. Guess if you want anything you're gonna have to go get it. Don't seem to be anyone offering any table service… At least for strangers."

"Don't really want anything, but I guess it would look funny if we just sat here."

I walked over to the bar. The dishwater blonde who waited on me either wasn't the wife in question or the deputies had some weird tastes. Fortyish, overweight, with a definite mustache, and poured into a blouse and jeans, neither of which were very clean, she asked, "Help you?" after letting me stand for a suitable time.

"Two tall Buds please… No glasses." I figured the bottle should be sanitary under the cap. Nothing else in the place looked that way.

"That'll be three fifty." Up front, before she made the trip to the cooler. Either being efficient or afraid I might disappear before she got back. I handed her a five, and when she returned with the beers she counted out my change on the bar, with nicotine stained fingers, and gave me a look that dared me to pick it up and not leave a tip.

In my usual intrepid way, I showed her by saying, "Keep it," and received a smile in return. It didn't ever quite make it above her nose. The eyes stayed cold and reptilian.

After I retreated to the table, Sherry said, "Talk about chicken. You don't think you're going to buy anything out of that one?" From there the conversation degenerated into occasional small talk as we attempted to overhear the conversation from the bar. They in turn were making sure we didn't, but must have turned to less interesting topics, because the pool players eventually returned to their game.

We sat idly watching the game with little conversation. The skinny guy sank one and Sherry said, "Nice shot." Her attempt at being friendly was not too effective. The guy merely grunted, and the big broad at the bar gripped her cue and looked daggers as if seeing Sherry as possible competition.

I changed my mind about challenging the table.

The mood was broken when four people, dressed same as the two pool players, came noisily in the door. They grouped around the others at the back end of the bar where there was a cooker, and ordered food to go with the beers that had been set up when they walked through the door. Must have been lunchtime at the fish cannery.

It was soon obvious the conversation was about us from the guarded looks thrown our way. After the barmaid had the food in the cooker, she broke a rule and came over to the table.

"They said you are a reporter?"

"Yeah...Sort of."

"Wouldn't want them to hear. You want anything else?"

"Not really. After last night it doesn't taste too good."

"Sure sign of an amateur." In a low voice, "I get off at five. Buy me a beer up at the Broken Oar?"

"It's a date." Then to Sherry as the woman walked away, "Never can tell what you can buy. Wonder what she wants?"

"Reporter, huh?" I looked up to see the hulk leaning on her cue across the table. The odor was partly explained. The front of her slicker was liberally decorated with glittering fish scales. She obviously had been here drinking a long time. "People come around here asking questions sometimes get hurt. Just a word of advice. Sometimes real bad hurt." She slapped the butt of her cue into her other hand a couple of times to punctuate the warning before she turned her back on us and returned to the pool table.

I took it as a hint. We left the two untasted beers on the table and made an almost dignified exit. I thought of putting a note on mine stating I had spit in it, but wasn't sure how many of the Safehaven patrons would be able to read it.

CHAPTER THREE

Back at the Gull, I flipped on my computer to warm up while I brewed another pot. I was going to call Charley and give him what I had, so with Sherry watching over my shoulder I began listing what we knew. The list wasn't very long, definitely not very impressive, even with both our best efforts.

I dug the phone out of the unmade bed and called Bernie instead. He wasn't at the station so I tried his home. His wife, sounding doubtful, said he was in the shower getting ready to try to catch up a little sleep, but she would ask. Bernie picked up the bedroom extension. I could still hear the sound of soft music from the other phone so figured she was still on. He grunted, "Yeah."

"This is your favorite reporter… Won't keep you from your beauty sleep very long… God knows you probably need it after all of the help you've had."

"Ankus! If I'd known it was you we wouldn't be having this conversation. This thing happened just after I went to bed last night. I got up and took the call and been at it ever since. I don't work too good without my sleep."

"Sorry buddy. Just wondering if there was anything new."

"No… County seems to have signed off on the Beasley kid. They are looking for him and not interested in looking much further."

"Told you I'd give you anything we picked up. So far it's damn little. Bunch of loonies out there beating the brush for him… Don't think they are much interested in bringing him in alive either. Lot of people out there think there is more to this thing than it appears. Lot of grumbling about the wife, and we smelled drugs in it too."

"That old Finn's drug of choice was booze. Fish all week and blotto all weekend. Hey… I don't want to be a hard nose but I'm standing here dripping all over the floor. I got to get some sleep."

"OK. Sorry. Hey, one more thing. Where do the kid's folks live? These dumb phone books…"

"You used that one on me before," he said with a sigh. "Guess if I'm gonna get you off the phone… Somewhere out Bear Valley road, big old house. You'll be able to spot it by all of the County cars staked out around it waiting for the kid to try to get home."

"Thanks Bernie. I owe you." He was gone without a further word.

"What's he got to say? Anything new?" from Sherry.

"Not really. The county has pretty much decided the Beasley kid is guilty so they aren't looking any further. Guess he has disappeared and both them and all of the red necks from the tavern are out beating the bushes trying to find him."

"They'd both probably shoot first and joke about it."

"Bernie says the family lives out Bear Valley… That's only about ten miles… Maybe we should drive out."

"Let me have the phone a minute. I'm going to call Judge Harriman." After dialing she sat and waited. I could see the resolve evaporating as she listened to the phone ring, then, "Oh… Judge Harriman. This is Sherry Thompkins, sorry to bother you at home."

After a pause, a one sided conversation, broken by faint scratches from the phone, "It's about this homicide… This Beasley Kid… The local rednecks have decided he is the one that did it and they are all out chasing him through the woods with guns… But judge… He isn't real smart… Diminished responsibility… Maybe someone could talk him

into coming in before he gets shot… That's not what I meant Judge…
OK, Thanks, I guess. I'll see the family and see what I can do."

"What was that all about?"

"Judge just appointed me to represent the kid. Now we have legal standing."

"Oh… It turns me on when you use that lawyer talk."

Bear Valley is a single lane blacktop angling off east from Highway
101 a few miles north of Long Beach. Sherry downshifted and whipped
the car into the right turn, and then immediately anchored it. "Stupid
god damn." She left the rest hanging as she slid with squealing tires,
broadside up alongside the sheriff's car, sitting there with its blue light
lazily flashing.

The deputy slouched out of the car, hitched up his Sam Browne
belt, and said, "Road's closed ma'am."

"Why is it closed? The Beasleys live up there don't they?"

At his nod she added, "I'm S. J. Thompkins, Attorney. I've been
appointed to represent Jimmy and I need to talk to them."

"Sorry ma'am, I can't let anyone through… Sheriff's orders."

In a tone that left little doubt about her mood, she said, "I suggest
you get on your radio and get someone to amend those orders. If they
question it, tell them to call Judge Harriman. I warn you he isn't going
to be in a real good mood. His weekend has been interrupted two or
three times already with this mess."

He leaned in the car window and grabbed the radio mike. About
thirty seconds later he was back out of the car. "Sorry for the mix-up
ma'am. They said let you through. We got crazies running around the
logging roads with rifles and shotguns looking for the kid. They were
up there threatening to shoot up the Beasley's house a couple hours
back. You can go ahead."

Very coolly, Sherry said, "I can't go anywhere until you move your
car." I could see the little knot on her jaw that showed how hard she
was working to maintain that cool.

"Oh yeah… Sorry," as he headed to his car.

Poking her head out the window, she said, "I'd suggest you park your car somewhere besides the middle of that corner. One of those four wheelers come around here they may not have brakes as good as mine."

Beasley's house was a two story clapboard, with shed additions across the back causing it to resemble a salt box, the whole thing sitting atop a daylight basement of sorts, a series of posts, designed to raise it above high water of the winter tides. Common along the coastal streams. If the house had ever been painted, it was not discernible as we drew up in front. Two car bodies adorned the side yard and an assortment of parts leaned against the front. Two large dogs came out to greet us noisily, explaining the muddy prints that decorated the boards up alongside the outside stairway to what was probably the front door.

They looked friendly, even the one who put his paws atop the hood and slobbered on the windshield in front of my face, but I wasn't about to test it. The house looked deserted. Nothing moved except the dogs when Sherry hit the horn. Belaboring the obvious I said, "Don't look like anyone is here. No pickup truck around. This far out you don't go without wheels."

"I thought that deputy said they were here," she said as she whipped the car around and threaded her way back toward the highway. The law had taken her advice and moved out where he was visible from highway 101. She pulled along side and asked, "I thought you said they were home?"

"Damn. Excuse the French ma'am, they were. We got another car up the other side and nothing has gone by there or I would have heard. These damn logging roads. It's like trying to keep a spider in the middle of his web. If you know your way around, you can go all over the county… Three counties actually… Without ever seeing the blacktop. These people grew up in these woods so they know all of the logging roads better than we do."

"Guess we will go back up and look around," she said as she put the car into reverse, backed around, and headed back up Bear Valley Road. We cruised by the house again, but nothing had changed, even the dogs who followed us up the road barking, until she increased the speed. We passed several barely visible old logging roads that angled off into the trees. Occasionally one would have a weathered wooden sign with something faintly readable, such as H-12 on it. Some had newer looking metal gates across, but with evidence of four-wheel rigs creating their own passage around them. None of the roads showed signs of recent use.

Some six or eight miles up we met the other sheriff's car heading down. Sherry pulled to the side and he stopped alongside. "See anything?" he asked. At our headshakes, he said, "Me too. It's like chasing smoke. I only been with the department a couple months. If I took off trying to find him on those logging roads the sheriff would probably have to send someone out to rescue me."

We found the first deputy back at the Beasley house. He was out of his car. The muddy footprint on his jacket sleeve bore witness to the fact that the dogs were truly friendly. It was when he walked up next to our car that I noticed the Sergeant's stripes on his arm and, looking across through Sherry's window, that he was so big I could only see his belt and the huge gun it supported.

We followed the lead of the second deputy when he pulled up and stayed in his car. After some small talk and the men agreeing to the futility of trying to find the absent family, I reminded Sherry we had a date in town. "You find Jimmy, I want to be notified. I want to be there before you do any questioning," she said to the Sergeant, and fired up the Z.

"Stop over there by the corner while I grab a couple quick shots of the cops guarding the place," I said as I dug the camera bag out from under my legs.

We were five minutes late at the Broken Oar. It is a huge barn of a place, planned to handle the summer tourist crowds. Never really understood why the people would drive a hundred miles to spend the whole weekend in a tavern. They could do that at home. We paused inside the door to let our eyes adjust to the dim light.

The bar ran down the wall on our right. There were two pool tables on the left, and probably twenty tables between. Toward the rear was a large dance floor and bandstand, with booths down each side of the room. The twenty or so mortals in attendance for happy hour were lost in the vastness. Apparently no one had yet attained happiness as all were pretty quiet, laughter was strained, and as if guilty, most looked up whenever the door opened, checking out the newly arrived.

"I don't see our friend. Have we been stood up or is she just late?"

Unable to pass up an opening like that, Sherry said in a saccharine voice, "She's probably late because of all those tips she has to count."

"Why don't you be nice and grab a table back there some place. I'll snag a couple of beers on the way." I placed the beers on the table in front of her and said, "I'll check out the booths in back to make sure she isn't hiding out." I walked back to the rest room in the rear and after a suitable interval returned. There was no one in any of the booths.

We sat, sipping our beer and exchanging snide comments about the patrons, but agreed that even though they were mostly candidates for Alcoholics Anonymous, they were a cut above those at the Safehaven.

She came in by the side door behind me. I became aware when Sherry half stood and motioned her over. I untangled my legs and stood and did the introductions. "This is Sherry, I'm Tom." She said her name was Helen. I asked, "What you drinking?"

"A wine cooler... Any kind... If that's Ok," she said, delivered in a hesitant way.

We sipped and chatted for a while. Helen ducked every time the door would open as if she were afraid of being caught consorting with the enemy. Finally, Sherry the lawyer took over. "How long have you worked at the Safehaven?"

"Just over three years. Melanie started more than a year after me." The tone of voice made my ears perk up.

"How long they been a thing? What's his name, the owner?"

"Jack Younger. They were uh, friends, before she went to work. At first I was afraid she was my replacement, but guess he didn't want her tied down that much."

"Her husband ever object?"

"Oh, she wasn't married to Suolo then. He was a regular. Was in whenever he was in port. I was surprised when she took up with him. He was such a weirdo. He would come in almost every week and get falling down drunk. He has a boat in the moorage you know. Worth a couple hundred thousand dollars I heard. I thought maybe that was the attraction. I'm not sure, but I think Jack put her up to the marriage."

I was still getting vibes, and asked, "What do you mean put her up to it? What gave you that idea?"

She held up her drink and said, "I'm getting dry." I raised up and signaled the bartender to bring three more, so as to not slow down the story. In typical drinker's fashion she picked up as if there were no interruption. "Jack used to get pissed if she got too friendly with any of the guys when she was tending bar, but never said a word about Suolo."

I let Sherry continue; she was asking the right questions, probably better than I would have done, and the woman to woman thing seemed to be working. "When did they get married?"

"Year... Eighteen months. Not sure it was much of a marriage though. Him gone four or five days at a time. When he was in he was usually drunk. He did clean up a little bit at first, but I'm not sure she ever spent many nights in his trailer and I'm sure she was never on his boat. She was always into anything for a high, but he was death on drugs. Course he didn't consider alcohol a drug. They used to get into some real fights over it."

"Jack always kept a bottle of grain alcohol stashed in the back. When they wanted to get rid of him, they would spike Suolo's beer so he would pass out quicker, then send him home in a cab."

"You hear anything lately? I mean since the killing or the past few days especially?"

"I walked into the office to get some change the other day. They shut up right away when they heard me, but not before I heard the word, insurance. Oh, and one of the guys was bragging this morning that he was Mr. Anonymous. Said Jack sent him out to call 911 from a pay phone, to report he heard the Beasley kid had done Suolo in. Real proud of it 'til Jack told him to keep his mouth shut or the cops would probably be around and grab him."

We told her I had a deadline to make and I dropped a five on the table and told her to have another. Before we got away, she made us promise we wouldn't mention her visit or her helping to anyone. She said because she was afraid for her job, but something didn't feel right about it.

Back at the car, Sherry said, "Real nice people. I can't imagine her being so worried about a job in that hole. Wonder how much of that was spite. Maybe she had ideas about Younger before Melanie came on scene."

"Is that lawyer or is it women's instinct?" Seeing the clouds gathering, I added, "You did real good with her," before the storm hit. I wondered why little Helen had met with us at all. I couldn't see any way she would profit and she obviously wouldn't get involved out of civic duty. What were her reasons for putting the monkey on Melannie's back if it wasn't jealousy? "Can you believe someone would actually get that worked up over a job at that place?"

"Small people usually have small ambitions," Sherry answered.

CHAPTER FOUR

When we added what we learned from the barmaid and the bits from the bakery to the file we had before, it still added up to slightly more than nothing. Lots of suspicions, almost no facts, but I decided to call Charley. By the third ring I knew I was going to get his machine and was tempted to hang up. I knew if I did he was bound to come in late and find my number on his machine and wake me up, or just as bad, call me again at the crack of dawn. The machine picked up half way through the fourth ring and I sat and listened to Charley's bored voice on tape.

At the beep, I said, "Damn Charley, you know how I hate talking to some dumb machine. This is Tom Hill. I've spent all day on this and don't have a hell of a lot of fact. The County Prosecutor is sure it is a kid named Jimmy Beasley, but I wouldn't go with that without a direct quote. He had a wife who stands to make about a quarter mil besides possibly some insurance, and is the hands down pick of most of the local gossip. She has a boyfriend who looks about as slimy as a slug, who owns the tavern this whole mess appears to be connected to. There is talk of spiked drinks, and drugs that neither the deceased nor the suspect appears to be into. The kid used a splitting maul apparently, but the cops are being tight mouthed about whether that is what actually did the guy in. Won't know for sure until they do the autopsy."

"The County boys don't have Beasley yet. He lit out for the woods and they haven't caught up with him. The vigilantes, some of the upright patrons of the bar where the wife works, are out with shotguns and rifles beating the bushes for him also. They probably know the woods better than the deputies so they are more apt to find him, if their booze supply doesn't run out first. I'm not sure they want him to come in alive. I'm sure they figure that if he suddenly becomes dead, the investigation will stop. We are going out tonight to mingle with some of these refined people. Maybe late getting home so it would be nice if we could sleep in a bit tomorrow morning. Night Charley." I hung on for a short moment before I cradled the phone, to see if Charley had been listening and would pick up.

"You plan to feed me before we go out and get our heads bashed? We haven't had anything all day except those doughnuts this morning. It's no wonder you got bones sticking out all over, you never think of eating."

"What do you mean…? I feed you… You're the only one around here working on a sure thing. You will bill the county for all your time today. I still don't have a guarantee that Charley won't send someone else over here Monday and stiff me."

"He couldn't do that."

"Why not?"

"We could sue him?"

"How? You are the only lawyer I know and you are my only witness. How you handle both?"

It was full dark when we got to the Bay View, a small neighborhood café with fairly good food and almost reasonable prices. Except during the tourist season when the prices go up and it's always crowded and noisy and I swear the food quality drops off considerably. The name is a misnomer also; it's about three blocks to the bay. It does have a view of a boat storage yard across the street if that counts for anything.

Tonight there were only two other tables occupied. The well

upholstered blonde behind the counter put down her paper, flashed a cheery smile, said, "Hello Tom," and followed us to a table with the coffee pot in hand. As she poured, she said, "You know honey... Until you came along I thought I might have a chance of snuggling up to that bony frame of his some night."

Seeing no response that would bring me out a winner, I said, "Hi Doris," and asked, "What you got tonight that's good?"

"You mean to eat?" she asked with a nasty laugh. "Chicken fry is probably good as anything."

"Bring us a couple. French fries. Blue cheese dressing."

"Yuk. Not for me. Make mine ranch." As Doris headed off toward the kitchen with the order, Sherry added, "She isn't kidding. I'm sure she'd like a chance to climb your frame."

"I'll have to keep it in mind, just in case the winter turns cold."

Lingering over coffee, we finally got around to what we should do next. With a full stomach, I could have been convinced to call it a day, but we agreed the answers were probably at the Safehaven Tavern. It was still early which was just as well because beer is always the farthest thing from my mind after eating. Doris made another of her frequent trips with the pot and I asked if she had heard anything about the murder.

"What makes you think I would know anything?" At my innocent shrug, she relaxed and said, "Only what I hear when I'm waiting table." What she told us was the same as we had heard elsewhere and she didn't seem to be too interested in discussing it. Probably a bunch of the Safehaven crowd were her regular customers also.

To put it off for a while longer, I said, "Maybe we should drive out past the Beasley place again and see if they are home."

We headed out north on 101 and Sherry gingerly turned on to Bear Valley Road, expecting to find a county car blocking it but the road was open. As we rounded the last curve before the house, there were parking lights beside the road. They turned to red and blue flashing as the deputy hit his overheads. She pulled up alongside and we were met by the beam from a flashlight in our faces. The man said, "Evening ma'am," and turned off his flashers and his dome light on.

Recognizing the man from earlier she said, "You still here? You put in some long hours."

"Short on deputies. I sent Wilson home to get a little sleep and moved back here where I can see the house."

"Anybody home yet?"

"The old man came back about dark. I think the wife has been there all the time."

"Guess I'll go see if they will talk to me. I'm going to try to get Jimmy to turn himself in before those crazies catch up with him."

"That and it can't be too comfortable out there. Sleeping in the truck I assume and it's gonna get cold as hell… Er…excuse me."

The dogs were in at least, for when we parked in front of the house I could hear them sounding the alarm. As I started up the stairs a light came on above us and I found Sherry right on my heels.

When I rapped on the door a man's voice, sounding none too friendly asked, "Who are you and what you want?"

Sherry took the lead. "Mr Beasley, I'm S. J. Thompkins, Attorney. Judge Harriman appointed me to help Jimmy. Can we talk to you for a minute."

"Why don't everybody just leave him alone?"

"Mr. Beasley, you know he is in trouble and they won't let him alone. If he stays out there in the woods, those crazies will eventually catch up with him and you know they aren't out to help him."

We heard voices through the door, obviously arguing. The dogs had shut up, but I could hear them snuffling at the crack under the door. Sherry was about to speak again when the door was opened by a red-eyed woman in a faded housedress. She was probably in her mid-forties, but life had not been easy for her. Gray haired, face deeply creased, and thin as a rail, she looked at least ten years older. She said, "Come in," in a voice that said she was not in the habit of making decisions or questioning her husband's decisions, and wasn't sure she was right to do so now.

Sherry stepped forward and put a hand on the older lady's arm and said, "Thank you. We only want to help Jimmy. I am afraid of what will happen to him if he stays out there in the woods."

"That's what I been telling Jim. Oh, where are my manners? This is my husband Jim and I'm Effie."

"I'm Sherry Thompkins, and this is my friend Tom Hill."

As I stepped through the door, the largest of the dogs, some sort of German Shepherd mix, decided to prove how friendly he was. I was almost knocked back down the steps when he placed two giant paws on my chest and drew a dripping tongue across my throat. Getting me separated from the dog and my neck dried off broke the ice.

Effie said, "Dern fool dogs. Come in and sit. Can I get you some coffee?"

Jim stuck out a gnarled hand and crunched my fingers, and said, "Sorry we was so unfriendly, but it's been a long day." He parked his lanky frame in a worn platform rocker, located strategically near the wood stove that had the room overly warm. He began stroking the stubble on his chin between his thumb and fingers as he slowly rocked. The big friendly dog flopped down alongside of his chair, but the other kept patrolling the room, obviously keeping an eye on us.

Jim's thin lips framed brown decayed teeth and his hawk beak nose appeared to be the only sharp thing about him. I'd put his age at late forties.

I looked around the sparsely furnished room. It went with the outside of the house, except it was scrupulously clean. There was little evidence of paint, but it looked as if it had all been scrubbed off by Effie's attempts at keeping it clean. The fir floors were bare except for a large, circular, hand-hooked rug that appeared to be made of hand-woven denim.

I was sloshing already, but figured it would make things even more friendly, so said, "Make mine black." Sherry nodded agreement. Effie brought the pot, with two mugs dangling from her other hand. She poured us a cup and refreshed theirs. From the smell it had been coffee for a long time, and it was definitely black.

Sherry opened with, "I spoke to Judge Harriman this afternoon and he is worried that Jimmy will get hurt out there in the woods with people hunting him with guns. These guys seem to consider it some sort of sport, and there is no guarantee one of the deputies won't shoot him if he tries to run." She paused to let this sink in. Jim was slowly nodding as if he were mulling it over. Effie was silently crying.

Turning to Jim, Sherry asked, "You know where he is don't you?" When he didn't answer right away she said, "We've got to get him…"

Effie cut her off with, "Please Jim."

"I don't know… He's so scared. I don't know if he will agree to come in."

Trying a different tack, I asked, "Did he tell you what happened last night."

"Not much. Like I said, he was so scared. He said somebody told him that crazy Finn was going to take that beat up old pickup away from him. He worked for Suolo for months and that was his only pay… Probably shoulda earned two three times what the truck is worth. Said he went there to ask Suolo about it and he just lay there in bed grinning at him and wouldn't even answer. He picked up a splitting maul that was there and threw it at him and ran. He is still more worried about losing that beat up old truck than he is about the rest of it."

Sherry said, "Maybe that is the way. We tell him the Judge sent me out here to see nobody takes the truck."

Jim shook his head as if he didn't like the idea, but before he could open his mouth, Effie repeated, "Please Jim. I don't want him hurt."

"You know they will lock him up?"

"I don't care… Least he won't get killed."

"Last time they had him in jail, those other guys wasn't too good to him."

"He's used to that. They always picked on him, even in school. Just cause he is a little slow."

The lawyer took over. Sherry said, "This is how we will do it. I will go out with Jim in his truck. First, I'll make a deal with the deputy. He waits here. When we get back, Jimmy will go with him, but only after he agrees to make sure Jimmy is kept by himself. I'll remind him the Judge sent me to see he doesn't get hurt and there are sure to be some of the Safehaven crowd in the jail. Always is. I'll ride back with Jimmy in his pickup and he can lock it up here and I'll make sure he gets the title straightened out so they can't take it away from him."

Jim was still shaking his head doubtfully, still thinking it through. Effie said, "Please Jim. He is out there all alone. I'm afraid he is going to get hurt… Or worse."

As if it were already decided, I said, "Sounds like a good plan. I think I should go along. Extra witness. How long do you think it will take us to find him?"

Jim, still acting as if things were moving faster than his brain, said, "Not too long. Before I took the long way 'cause I didn't want to be followed. He ain't far from here."

Sherry said, "I'm going to go and tell the deputy. I'm sure he is going to want to argue about it."

"I'll tag along. Like to see how you handle a deputy. I never had too much luck myself."

She did just that. Handled the deputy that is. Out of the light from the house, with our eyes used to the inside, the night was blacker than the coffee Effie had just served. We stumbled the short distance to the county car and Sherry rapped on the window. The startled Deputy opened the door and turned on the dome light.

Sherry said, "We've got a deal for you. Mr. Beasley thinks he may know where Jimmy is hiding. He is going to take us out and if he can find him we will try to talk him into coming back down here with us and he will surrender to you."

"I think maybe I should just go out with Mr. Beasley and bring him back. Won't be any question of him wanting to come back."

"You did hear what I said. I said Mr. Beasley thinks maybe he knows where he is. You insist on going along, how much chance you think there is he will be able to find him?"

"I could arrest him for harboring."

"Sergeant, we both want the same thing. You want him in jail and I want him where he won't get hurt. Judge Harriman sent me out here to see he doesn't get hurt. You wait here about an hour and you can take him back to South Bend and be the hero, and then go home and get some sleep."

"That last part sounds good… The sleep, that is…. OK, We'll do it your way. Guess I haven't got much to lose."

Feeling a victory, Sherry bored in on him and said, "This is the way it will be. We will bring him back here. He will lock up his truck and get a few minutes with his mother, then we will bring him over to the car. Oh yes… When you get to the jail, you will see he gets a cell by himself? There are always some of the rough crowd in there and I have reason to believe they may try to get to him."

Sarcastically, "Yes ma'am. Anything else? Maybe we should order in some food for him."

As she turned on her heel, she threw back, "That might not be a bad idea. He is sure to be hungry after being out there all this time."

Figuring she didn't know when to quit while she was ahead, I said, "You go get Jim, I want to talk to the Sergeant a minute." Dragging out my notebook in my best reporter style, I said, "I'll see you get credit for bringing him in. What is your name?"

"Sergeant Malahovsky, and I'm not too worried about getting credit."

"Malahovsky? Another good Finn name? How you spell that?"

"Polish," he said, daring me to comment. "Just like it sounds." He proceeded to spell it anyway, and then spelled Steven as if he were dealing with a mental midget. I got the feeling it was pay back for my witnessing his loss of face in the exchange with Sherry.

CHAPTER FIVE

The rains had stopped. The breeze off the bay was fresh, and almost balmy. The faintly fishy smell indicated the tide must be out. I helped Sherry up into the cab of the F-250 four-wheel drive with the jacked up frame and the oversize tires, and then climbed up myself. I barely got the door closed when Jim roared out onto the blacktop with smoking tires. The change from the slow talking meek man of a few moments ago was startling. Bracing one hand on the dash, I looked out the back and asked him what he would do if the deputy decided to follow.

"He won't. He knows that dinky little car couldn't keep up off the blacktop."

Some five minutes up the road on which we had met the other deputy earlier, he hung a quick right and we were barreling down on one of the steel gates erected by the timber companies to keep out the public. At about fifty feet, when I had braced for the inevitable crash, he swung left up the side of the hill and we were immediately blinded by the tree limbs wrapping over the windshield and cutting off the light by slapping the headlights as we climbed the steep bank. At the crest he turned right, with one wheel running over the top and the other still on the side of the hill, for about two heartbeats, and then it was right again and we careened down the hill. A quick left and we were back on the logging road with the gate still intact but behind us. All of this in total darkness except for the headlights and they were blinded by the trees a good share of the way. Obviously he had been this way before.

I looked at Sherry. She was sitting stiffly erect with eyes wide and mouth slightly ajar like she had quit breathing. I furtively ran a hand across the seat under myself to make sure I hadn't lost any of the coffee I had consumed earlier. Once I let the thought into my head, I began hoping we wouldn't be long. I didn't think Jim would be interested in making the pit stop I suddenly needed.

"I see what you mean. About the deputy following us in his car I mean," I said as I turned to look out the rear window again. Before we turned the first corner I was rewarded by the sight of the bars of the gate, outlined by the headlights of a car. The deputy obviously had followed us with lights out until he was stopped by the gate.

Jim hunched over the wheel, concentrating on the rutted and rocky road, for possibly another five miles, then turned left up a hill, on an almost invisible track that appeared to be a much older logging road as the trees had grown to almost cover it. After a climb of about half a mile we emerged onto what had obviously been a logging landing, but so long ago it was now almost grown over. He stopped and honked the horn, two short and one long, and announced, "We wait here."

I said, "Be right back," and slipped out to take care of my most pressing problem. When I opened the door the light was blinding and when I returned and opened the door to reenter the truck, the dome light again destroyed our night vision.

"You probably scared him. He could see too many people," as Jim hit the horn again, two short and one long. After some two or three minutes, he did it again and finally a shadow appeared at the left side of the truck. The slight figure, obviously poised for flight, held a crouched position about six feet from the truck. Jim softly said, "It's all right boy… They are friends come to help." He grunted at us, slipped out of the cab, and walked off into the darkness with the kid.

They were gone a long time. Long enough for my eyes to become adjusted to the darkness, enough so I could make out the outline of the trees against the cloud-darkened sky, but not enough to see the two people. Sherry finally asked, "You think he is going to be able to convince him to talk to us even?"

"If he's having this much trouble getting him to talk to us, how much chance you got talking him into going in?"

"It doesn't usually work like this. Usually my clients are already in jail and I am trying to get them out. He's got to understand it's dangerous out here, I have to convince him he could get hurt."

"I'm not sure that's the right tack. It doesn't sound like he is worried about anything out here, nothing except that damn truck."

The two Jims were suddenly standing beside the Ford. Sherry rolled the left window down and said, "Hello Jimmy," and held out a hand. He merely looked at it in distrust. She opened the door a crack, causing the light to go on. He stepped backwards quickly into the darkness, and crouched ready to run. After sitting in the dark for so long, the dim light was enough for us to see the boy clearly. He was a copy of his father. I would judge him at over six feet tall, but less than a hundred fifty pounds. The same nose, and in a few years he would have the same rotten teeth.

Sherry asked, "Jimmy, You know Judge Harriman don't you?"

"He put me in jail."

In a quick change of direction she asked, "Do you know there are men out here with guns trying to find you?"

"Dad said that."

"We think…Judge Harriman thinks… They want to hurt you." When this drew no response, she finally said, "We think they want to shoot you and take your truck."

"No! It's mine! I worked for it! I even fixed it so it runs better. It's mine." Then in a more normal voice, "The man said Mr. Suolo was going to take it back. I went and talked to him but he wouldn't talk to me."

"What man told you he was going to take it back?"

"The tavern man said."

During this exchange, Jimmy had relaxed. Sherry slid out onto the ground, standing inside the door with her right hand holding the bottom of the window that was at the height of her head. Jimmy fell back a step and resumed his runner's stance. She said, very softly, "Jimmy, we just want to help you. We'll see that no one takes your truck. I'll talk to Judge Harriman and ask him to fix a paper that says it is yours and then nobody can take it. But mostly we don't want to see you get hurt. Your mother is worried you will get hurt out here like this. She wants you to come home." He had relaxed partially again. Sherry took a half step forward and put her free hand very lightly on his arm. He crouched again like a wild animal, afraid of the touch but not wanting to break it.

His father chose this time to speak. He said, "That's right. Your mother wants you to come home. She has been crying all day because you are out here all alone and she is afraid something will hurt you."

"I come out here all the time. Nothing never hurts me."

The father said, "These are not things… These are guys, bad guys with guns. They want to find you and maybe kill you. We want you to come home before they hurt you. You don't like to see your mother cry."

Jimmy was shaking his head like things were moving faster than his brain was capable of understanding, but he had accepted Sherry's hand on his arm. After some small talk, she turned to me and said, "Jimmy, this is Tom Hill. He will go with us to see Judge Harriman."

When I slid out alongside her, he hardly moved. I stuck out a hand and said, "Glad to meet you Jimmy." He surprised me by taking my hand in a quick, limp, low pressure shake.

From there it was mostly downhill. I asked what really happened and he mumbled something unintelligible. I told him we had to know what happened so we would know what to tell the judge because they were saying he murdered Suolo. He was unimpressed. I tried to convince him we needed to know so we could help him find a place to go before the local vigilantes could hurt him.

He said, "They don't find me."

Sensing my growing frustration, Sherry finally said, "Jimmy, we are trying to help you." She added in a very soft voice. "We need to

40

know what happened before we go to see Judge Harriman. We can't get him to give us a paper that says nobody can take your truck if we don't know."

Again, it pushed the right button. He told the story in a disjointed fashion, sometimes wandering off in unexpected dead ends and stopping with a puzzled expression as he lost his way. Sherry would gently prod him and the monologue would begin again. I got the feeling he was speaking more words than he had used at one sitting in his entire life.

After about fifteen minutes, he had told us almost exactly what we had heard before from his dad and had pieced together for ourselves. Only on two points did his story add salient information. The first, Jack Younger had caught him at Oceanside's only service station and told him that Suolo had been at the tavern, laughing that he didn't need Jimmy to work anymore so he was going to take back the pickup. The other, he had gone by the trailer three times before he found the Finn at home about ten that night. On the third attempt he found Suolo in bed with the lights on, with his head propped up on pillows. He just lay there and grinned at him and wouldn't answer so he picked up the maul and threatened him. When he didn't respond, he threw it at him and ran.

At this point we had used about an hour and a half of the hour we had asked the deputy to wait. Sherry started prodding Jimmy to take his truck back to the house without too much luck. The senior Beasley finally said, "Jimmy your mother is sitting there crying because she is so worried about you being out here. You know you don't like to see her cry. You go get your truck and bring it up here, then follow us back to the house. We probably otta use the mainline out to the blacktop. Come in off 101. It's a little longer, but maybe the deputy is still waiting above the house."

Surprising everyone, Jimmy started off meekly to comply, and Sherry said, "We'll ride back with you. We want to make sure nobody tries to stop you on the way." Me, I was happy with the idea we were not going to have to make the trip around the gate again, but considering Jimmy's mental level, I wasn't too sure he would be an improvement.

We saw the headlights bobbing back in the trees, then the old truck came snorting and coughing up the hill and stopped beside the 250. As we walked toward the older pickup, Jim senior backed his 250 around where his lights picked it out. It was jacked up almost as high as the 250.

It was also a Ford four-wheel drive, probably late sixties, with a terminal case of coast cancer. There were holes rusted through both the rear fenders and the box. When I handed Sherry up into the cab, she said, "OOO…easy." I shortly learned what she meant. There were springs poking out from holes in the upholstery, both seat and seatback. The floor under my feet felt spongy and I suspected in daylight it would be possible to watch through the holes between your feet and see the road go by.

Once warmed up, the six-banger under the hood ran smoothly. It was obvious who had taught him to drive, as he had no trouble keeping up with his father who again was wasting no time. The old truck's headlights alternately played on the treetops and the road close in front as they flopped around in their sockets, and all of the sheet metal rattled and complained as we bounced over the ruts and rocks. Out on the black top of 101, except for the roar of the wind leaking around the windows and up through the floor, it settled down and sounded almost like a proper truck.

Jim proved to be right. Back at the house, the deputy was nowhere in evidence. He was apparently waiting on the road above for us to return. Jimmy pulled in at the end of the house by the two old hulks. By daylight his truck would probably fit right in. Sherry climbed down and said, "Nice truck Jimmy, why don't you lock it up so nobody can mess with it."

He said simply, "It won't lock, ma'am."

He barely hit the ground when he was wrapped in Effie's arms, at least the bottom half of him was. She was at least a foot shorter, but she was acting as if he were still her little baby. After the last hour, I was inclined to see her point. She said, "Oh Jimmy, I was so scared.. You being out there alone and all…."

"Oh, Maw, ain't nothing going to hurt me out there. Please don't cry. You know I don't like to see you cry," and he was crying too. If I hadn't been such a hardened old newspaperman, I might have joined them.

Effie started to ask if he were hungry, but before he could answer we were bathed in light as Sergeant Malahovsky slid to a stop in the gravel in front of the house. He immediately grabbed his gear and started to jump out of the car. Quick as he was, Sherry was quicker. She was standing alongside the car with one hand on the top of the doorframe and leaning over peering in the window. She held her ground and waited for him to open it. When he did so, she instantly went on the attack. "We had a deal. You were going to wait here, but you followed us."

Jimmy was crouched again as if to run, but his mother was holding his arm and talking to him in a low voice. The deputy who couldn't get out without knocking Sherry out of his way began to stammer. She said, "Slow down. We just got here. Give his mother a few minutes and she will bring him over. Don't you ever do anything the easy way?"

I moved over to talk with the deputy and Sherry went to assist Effie with talking Jimmy into going to jail. I asked if he had heard anything new on the victim. He slowly pushed the door open and stood up, stretching as if he were saddle sore, and with his eyes on the others, said, "Not very much. We don't talk too much on the radio. Too many people around with scanners, so I don't hear too much until I go in or call on the phone."

We both stood silently and watched as Jimmy gradually folded beneath the weight of the two women's arguments. Eventually the three walked over to the car and Sherry told the deputy that Jimmy was ready to go.

"Sorry ma'am… It's policy," as he made Jimmy stand with hands on the car roof while he frisked him, then cuffed his hands behind his back. He was almost gentle as he helped the lanky boy fold up into the tiny back seat.

Sherry said, "I was serious Sergeant. I want him in a separate cell because I am not sure somebody won't try to get rid of him so we will quit asking questions." To Jimmy she said, "I will be in tomorrow morning to see you. I don't want you to say anything to anybody about

Suolo unless I am there." She was looking directly at the deputy when she finished.

As he slipped into the front seat I said, "Well, you got your man and it looks like you will get some sleep tonight."

"Maybe… Maybe not. I may end up back down here watching this place all night. Those crazy drunks out there won't know we have the kid so they may still come back here and try to tear the place up."

"I think they will be all right. When we leave here we are going to drop by the Safehaven. Want to stir things up a little bit. We'll just let it slip that he is in your jail… Should draw the heat away from this place."

The deputy slowly said, "Safehaven… Yeah that would probably do it all right. But I'm not sure that is too smart on your part. I'd watch my backside in that place was I you."

We stood and watched the tail lights of the deputy's car recede around the corner toward the highway, then said goodbye to the Beasleys and hit the road toward home.

CHAPTER SIX

Business was good at the Safehaven, in part probably because of the murder. Because we had spent so much time out in the dark, the place looked almost bright, but the smell hadn't improved even a little bit. The chatter died away in a wave radiating out from us as we walked through the door and all eyes turned our way. The quiet became deafening. Not the thing to instill confidence in the less than heroic.

The only seating open was a booth under the front window. It was too far from most of the action for us to hear much, but we slid into it, glad for the refuge. The conversation picked up again, but most of the eyes were on us and I was sure we were the subject of most of the talk. This time we weren't ignored. The two reserve deputies were right. Melannie was a looker. There was no doubt of the identity of the well-stacked blonde who headed our way. Maybe twenty-eight, about five four, a hundred twenty pounds, in a tight green dress that exposed a lot of her at both ends. She asked, "Can I get you something?" in a honey voice with a phony Southern accent, but with a frozen smile that made me want to check my back to see if she could see someone behind me with a knife or a gun.

"Bring us a couple tall Buds, no glasses." As she started to move away I added, "Save yourself a walk," and handed her a bill.

I'm sure she wasn't out of earshot when Sherry said, "Had to call her back for another look… You know you are not going to get anything out of her. She sure is the perfect example of the grieving widow though."

When she returned with the beers and my change, it was obvious she had overheard as she began flirting with me. I took advantage to say, "You must be Melannie." When she agreed, I added, "We were talking to the county deputies a few minutes ago. They had the Beasley kid… The one supposed to have killed your husband. He was in their car and they were on their way to the South Bend Hilton with him."

She was good. The smile only faded a little bit around the edges, before she recovered and said very sweetly, "That's good. They finally got off their asses and locked him up before he could kill anyone else."

Sherry tossed in, "Yes…We were glad to see him in jail, before anyone got hurt," in a tone of voice that left her meaning open to interpretation.

The blonde didn't go directly behind the bar, she detoured past a group who had pushed two tables together near the back of the room. The conversation was animated and finally even Melannie could not resist sneaking a peak at us. "Suppose we could get an invite to that table? I'll bet it would sure answer a lot of our questions," from Sherry.

I guess Melannie decided she needed reinforcements as she came back toward us but continued on to enter a door behind Sherry in the corner, marked office. She was inside only about thirty seconds when she reappeared, followed by a man who had to be the slug I described to Charley. He walked nonchalantly in an arc that took him close enough to our table for him to get a good look as he made his way back to the same two tables.

I made him at fifty something, close to twice as old as Melanie. He obviously was one of his own better customers. His belt size, double mine, still only succeeded in holding his stomach up, not in. The pants it held up were almost as dirty as the shirt above. The stubble on his chin was maybe his attempt at Don Johnson, but on his porcine face, he'll never make it. As he swung near, where I could appreciate his sagging jowls, his thick lips, and his little beady eyes, I said, "Maybe I should apologize to the slugs." At Sherry's questioning look I added lamely, "The message I left on Charlie's machine."

She said, "Oh," with a pained expression, then after some time to consider it she said, "I guess I see what you mean. He really does look like something crawled out from under the house."

The volume gradually increased at the other end of the room but it tapered down to a murmur at the tables nearest to us. The result was a lot of noise but no intelligible voices. After fifteen minutes or so, it became clear that we weren't even going to be acknowledged again by the bartender. Against my better judgment I said, "Maybe I should go up to the bar and get us another beer... Sort of stir the pot a bit, get something started maybe."

"You sure that's a good idea? Maybe we should just get out of here while we are still healthy."

"I don't know, they are going to great lengths to ignore us. With this many drunks, someone has to have put out the word. I think it will take a few minutes for the word to change." I slid out of the booth and caught my foot on the table's center support and almost fell on my face. It brought the whole room to a standstill and every eye was on me as I crossed to the bar. Melannie was very carefully looking the other way.

Younger stood for a full minute, then said something to her. She started to move my way and I held up two fingers. She glanced at the slug. He said something in a low voice, and she snatched two tall Buds from the cooler and advanced on me, pausing half way down the bar to open them, on an opener under the bar. With a stiff smile she said, "Jack said they are on the house."

With a mock tip of the hat in his direction, I said, "Give the gentleman our thanks," and moved back across the room.

When I slid into the booth, Sherry asked, "What was that all about?" While I was telling her what had transpired, her eyes widened and she said, "My God... Look at that," and pointed her finger across my arm. Our acquaintance of our earlier trip was rising up out of a booth and it was obvious she had consumed her share in the hours since. Her skinny friend was lolling in the back corner. His eyes were open and staring. I wasn't sure if he was alive or if he had succumbed to an excess of alcohol and nobody had as yet noticed. It was like watching a sea lion fight her way up out of the water onto a rock. When she finally stood up, she shook herself, then turned and headed our way. That's when I noticed she still had her friendly pool cue in her hand. It looked ridiculously small, but definitely deadly.

She had to navigate around two vacant pool tables and I kept hoping she was intent on a game. No such luck. By the time she came past the last table, she had metamorphosed. She no longer looked like she had been drinking for twelve or more hours. Maybe more like four or five hours. She stopped a foot from the end of our table, placed her cue tip on the floor, put both hands on top of the butt, and stood looking at us. After what felt like a long time, she said, "You don't hear good." It didn't sound like a question.

Trying to keep my voice steady, I asked, "What didn't I hear?"

I was afraid I had blown it when she started to rise up, but she relaxed again and said, "I told you that people who come around here asking a lot of questions are apt to get hurt. Maybe bad hurt."

"But we didn't ask any questions. We just stopped to tell Melannie they had caught up with the Beasley kid. Thought she would like to know they had him in jail." That appeared to stop her. She turned and glanced toward the bar where she apparently received no signal. When she turned back she looked less sure of herself.

She started, "She didn't tell us…" when she was interrupted by her emaciated friend who had somehow revived and stumbled over and grabbed my arm. He said, "I told you this morning to leave my old lady alone. You come in here hitting on her and I'll deck you."

She said, "Cleave, you're drunk. You wouldn't know a deck if it came up and hit you in the ass. Nobody is hitting on me. Why don't you go back and sit down?"

"They can't come in here asking all these questions… You know what Younger said."

I wasn't too worried about Cleave. He was a lightweight, both physically and mentally, as well as having enough trouble trying to keep vertical that he wouldn't be a problem. But he was beginning to draw a crowd who were egging him on. I knew that whatever he started, his lady friend would have to take his side, and she obviously outweighed both him and me in both areas. The noises had now reversed. The table in the rear was almost silent and there were plenty of voices near enough for us to hear and understand them, but we didn't really want to hear what they were saying. Those at the rear gradually moved forward to join the fun, pushing the front row ever nearer to us.

Some dozen or so of the patrons formed an arc with the end of our table its center. I thought they looked like a film I had seen of the spectators at a cockfight, waiting for the sight of blood, as they voiced their support for Cleave. The press of the pack effectively cut off any hopes of our slipping out of the booth and reaching the door.

I looked toward the bar for support. It was obvious there would be none. Both Jack Younger and Mellannie were standing behind the near end of the bar, with palms on top supporting their weight, as they watched the action with apparent amusement. I got the feeling he would break into applause if some of our blood just happened to spill onto his grimy floor.

Sherry said, "I'd say you did a good job of stirring the pot. Can you do as well getting us out of here with all our pieces intact?"

I picked up my bottle and pretended to sip, reversing my grip so it could serve as a weapon if worse came to worse. Not much, but better than nothing. I told Sherry, "If something starts, I'll try to create a diversion. You duck under and get the hell out of here and bring the cops." I turned back toward the crowd. The hulk was actually trying to cool Cleave, but he was hearing the crowd and his ego was pressing him. He was so drunk it took a while for him to make his body and mind go the same way, but I could see it wouldn't be long. She would make three of him, but in true law of the redneck world, the man will always have the last say. If he said fight, she would do so.

I looked at the window and thought about throwing my bottle through it, and then diving after it. The window was big enough. Probably four feet high and six long, but the bottom was about four feet off the floor.

I'm not an expert on breaking glass, but I seem to remember they mostly break leaving jagged pieces around the edges. Especially the bottom edges that I would of a necessity be trying to traverse in a hurry.

"I asked you a question!" came from Cleave who was pressing forward menacingly.

"Sorry, guess I missed it with all the noise." Tensing my right leg while I tried to remember how the heroes consistently do it in the movies. Do I try to plant it in his face, or do I go for the always vulnerable but hard to hit kneecap? But then how do I dodge that pool cue in her hands when she comes to his aid, with me starting from a sitting position?

I didn't hear anything, but I became aware everyone's eyes had turned toward the door behind me and the room became quiet. I sneaked a look and sagged in relief. Who says there is never a cop around when you need one? Bernie and one of his reserve uniforms were standing just inside the door. As the crowd began to melt away Bernie made his way toward us. Cleave in his befuddled state, still hadn't noticed. He still pressed forward. She hissed, "Cops," and grabbed his arm and spun him toward the back of the tavern. She stopped, holding him with one hand, his feet half off the floor, and asked, "You told Melannie they had caught up with Jimmy Beasley?" At my nod, she looked toward the bar for a few seconds, then saying nothing further, moved her man toward their booth in the back. Younger was glaring his disappointment.

"Good evening Ankus... Counselor. You folks regular patrons of this fine establishment?"

"Hi Bernie. Never realized before how well I like your uniform. What brought you charging to the rescue?"

"Sgt. Malahovsky called and suggested we do a walk through if your car stayed in the parking lot for over a half hour. What kind of fool trick is this? Bringing her in here? And why did you try it anyhow?"

"Two reasons... First, to get these cretins off the Beasleys, and second, we thought we might find out some part of what happened. There is something involved in this mess, other than the kid and his truck."

Finally finding her voice, Sherry said, "I agree, that's a nice uniform.

50

But why don't we continue this conversation outside… I'm still not convinced your magic will hold forever."

Bernie backed a step, bowed, and motioned Sherry ahead of him toward the door. I waited for her to pass, turned and tipped my nonexistent hat toward the two behind the bar again, and followed her out. The weather was still holding. It had cooled off considerably, but was still not raining. We stood in the parking lot and talked. I asked Bernie if there had been anything new.

He said, "No, and there won't be until we get the results of the autopsy. All I really know is the Finn was found with a splitting maul sticking in the side of his head and the hospital took a blood sample before they shipped him to Portland. He had a blood alcohol level somewhere up around point four. That's a lethal dose for anything but a confirmed alcoholic you know."

Sherry said, "That ties in with what the barmaid told us." At Bernie's questioning look she added, "She told us that Melannie and Younger kept a bottle of straight alcohol in the back room so when they wanted to get rid of Suolo for the night, they would sweeten his drinks so he would pass out, then send him home in a cab."

"Real pair of sweethearts. It's late, maybe we should get together in the morning and sort of compare notes."

His voice didn't sound as if he were saying the same thing his words said, but I agreed it was getting late, and said, "Thanks again for coming to the rescue… I think I know how the settlers felt when the cavalry came riding over the hill after the Indians already had the wagon train encircled."

Sherry said, "We can talk, but just remember, I represent Jimmy Beasley so some of what I know I may not be able to talk about."

"That's all right Counselor. Just remember, Ankus here was with you all day and saw and heard the same things you did. He doesn't have any client or immunity. Goodnight. Pleasant dreams."

"And I was getting to like you and now you go all cop on us." When he shrugged and started to walk away, she added, "We are afraid they are going to try to get to Jimmy Beasley in the jail. If you could suggest to the guys up at South Bend that they keep an eye out, I would appreciate it." We were not even sure he heard, as he grunted and stuffed himself into the compact police car and hit the starter. Feeling rather lonely with him gone from the dark parking lot, we wasted no time before following suit.

CHAPTER SEVEN

After the short drive, Sherry wheeled into the Gull parking lot, and turned off the Z. Nobody said a word. We both slumped back exhausted. It was hard to believe it was still the same day as Charley's wake-up call. Jim Beasley was right; it had definitely been a long one.

I finally said, "I'd be in favor of just sleeping right here, but I know morning would be hell. Besides I need a shower after that joint." As I opened the door and unfolded, I became aware my phone was ringing and heading for the door said, "Five gets you ten it's Charley."

It rang again as I pushed the door open and hit the wall switch. When nothing happened I remembered I had been intending to replace the burned out overhead light bulb for the past two weeks. I cussed when I couldn't remember where we left the phone and I couldn't find it in the dim light from the street. It finally dawned on me, the reason I couldn't find it was because it had quit ringing.

When I finally found a light, Sherry behind me said, "It could only be Charley, why don't you call him back?"

"I'm not sure I'm ready to talk to him. What have we actually found out that is more than a guess since I talked to his machine this afternoon?"

"We got Jimmy where those loonies can't get him." She hugged herself, shivered, and added, "God! Now I know how a mouse feels when a cat has him and is toying with him before he gets around to eating him. The hungry looks on those faces when they were ringed around us…. I'll have nightmares for the next month."

I hit the switch on my computer and checked the coffee pot while I waited. Any thoughts of nuking the leftovers faded when I found we had forgotten to turn it off and what was left was a dark brown band around the carafe and a half inch of liquid that resembled chocolate syrup, but definitely didn't smell like it. Since it looked like a long night, I scrubbed out the pot and started another. I found myself scraping the bottom of the can, so I made a mental note to pick up another can of coffee when I went to buy the light bulbs.

Calling up the file, I said, "We really don't have much. The Finn got done… Anonymous says the Beasley kid did it… The kid is hiding out in the hills… The people at the Safehaven don't like us except the other barmaid, and I suspect her motives. Other than suspicions, not much. She told us they were feeding Suolo alcohol and talking about insurance. How much can we believe? What's in it for her? She wouldn't volunteer unless she had an axe to grind."

I turned to Sherry and found she had kicked off her shoes, piled the pillows against the head of the bed, and was lying back about half asleep. She said, "We can add Jimmy Beasley admits to hitting him with the maul…. And he's in jail. And Bernie said the Finn had enough alcohol in his system to kill him."

I punched that in and said, "And the kid said Younger was the one who set him off. And the guy at his joint who made the call was Mr. Anonymous."

Getting into the spirit, Sherry said, "If we can believe… What did she say her name was? Helen… We never did get a last name did we?" At my blank look, she went on, "She had a lot of nasty stuff to say, but mostly it aimed at Melannie, not so much Younger. I agree… I wonder about her motives."

"Maybe you're right, I never could see inside a woman's head, and about half of what we have is based on what she told us."

"Just from their attitude, Younger and Melannie have to have something going on.... And all those people in the tavern getting all up in arms when they think someone is asking questions or checking up.... That had to be orchestrated by somebody."

"Not necessarily. You've led a sheltered life. That's a whole 'nother culture.... Did a feature on it once. I mean people whose lives are the tavern. They are just naturally leery of outsiders... People who can live without alcohol are not to be trusted. Probably at least half of that bunch at the Safehaven are regulars at the South Bend Hotel. Drunk driving...fighting...petty theft to support their habits...drugs; they don't have any life other than the tavern. And sadly, they raise their kids to be the same."

"So you don't think Younger was telling them what to do? How much of what we heard can we believe?"

"It's not quite that simple. To the tavern crowd, the tavern owner is some kind of god. He is in the position of controlling their lives, or at least their booze, which is some place ahead of oxygen in importance. He can bar them from the place and not only cut them off from their friends, not to mention the embarrassment, but he can deny them the alcohol without which they can't live. He doesn't have to tell them what to do. They see us as a threat to him and do what they think would get them closer to him by helping out. End of lecture... I don't know if all of that made any sense." The smell of fresh cooked coffee finally reminded me so I rinsed out and refilled the morning cups.

Sherry nodded her thanks when I handed her a cup and took a slow sip of the hot and black before saying, "Suppose you are right. Where does that leave us... How much of all of this can we believe?"

"I don't know really. The insurance stuff, and how much Suolo was worth, and who benefits... We can't find out about any of that until Monday. Probably be the middle of the week before they get the autopsy reports. You know, I'd like to talk to that big old gal away from the tavern and sober. And without Cleave."

"Like that do you? You better watch yourself you go hitting on Cleave's girl."

"No… Just for a minute there… She was showing some intelligence. She was wondering if she were being used… Even with as much booze as she was obviously carrying."

"I have to admit, about that time my mind wasn't working along that direction. I was too scared. I don't like the sight of blood and I was afraid I was going to see some. Unfortunately ours."

I scrolled through the file again. There really wasn't much more concrete fact than we had before. I said, "We covered a lot of ground today, but I'm damned if I know what any of it means. Wonder if Charley has heard anything?" Then answering my own question, "I don't know how he could. This happening on a Saturday and all. All of the big guns he could be talking to aren't going to let the departure of a drunken fisherman interrupt their weekend. If I don't call him he will wake us up again in the morning… If I do he will keep me on the phone half the night and still maybe wake us up in the morning."

Turning toward me she sat up on the edge of the bed, took a sip of her coffee, set the half full cup on the night stand and said, "I'm bushed. Think I will grab a shower and turn in. You do whatever." Seeing my eyes light up she added, "Forget it Romeo, I said I was tired. And before you ask, I don't need anyone to wash my back."

I watched her disappear into the bathroom and then turned back to the computer. There had to be something there I was missing. The sound of water in the shower was distracting as hell, and my brain like Sherry's was still wrestling with the thing at the tavern. When the water sounds quit, I shut it down, turned off the coffee pot and all of the lights except the bed lamp. The door opened and I groaned. Sherry had donned one of my T-shirts. It didn't hide much. The top half was tight and only accented instead of hiding, and the bottom half was a few inches short of hiding. Her normally long legs seemed to go on forever. All the way from the floor up to heaven.

She said, "Down boy." Then proceeded to deliberately bend over and pull the covers down, and sit down on the edge of the bed facing me. Both actions accomplished what she intended.

I said, "I'll be right there," and headed for the shower, as I watched her pull the covers up so all that was visible was a swatch of auburn

MAULED

hair. A short ten minutes later I slid in beside her.

I put one arm over her and she rolled over and put her head on my shoulder. I became aware she was shivering as if she were cold. She said, "Just hold me," and moved as tight against me as possible. "I was so scared… I'll never forget the expressions on their faces." She finally drifted off to sleep, but it was a long time before she quit twitching. My arm under her lost all feeling, but I was afraid to move it. I finally joined her, both in sleep and the unpleasant dreams.

Then I became aware of the elbow in my back and heard, "Answer the dumb phone."

I located the phone under the edge of the bed, picked up the receiver, and ducked back under the covers out of the cold. I could see the normal coast weather had returned by the rivulets of water coursing down the window. The damp cold had seeped in while we slept. I said, "Hi Charley…"

He cut me off with, "Why the hell don't you get an answering machine? I rang your phone every half hour for half the damn night last night and never did get you."

"You know I don't like to talk to a machine, and I don't think I want one talking for me, even more so." I didn't tell him I heard his call. Just, "I told you we were going to the Safehaven Tavern last night. We didn't get in until almost midnight."

"So what did you learn?"

"Not all that much, beyond that they really don't like us." I proceeded to give him a run down, and then added, "What it amounts to is we have a lot of suspicions, but not much fact."

"You're going to have something for me today aren't you?"

"Yes… I'll have something for you by this evening. We have a date with the local officers…at their request…for this morning. They are the ones gave me the information on the Finn having enough alcohol in him to be dead."

Sounding a bit more relaxed, Charley repeated, "Just don't dump a mess of stuff on me at deadline."

57

"OK Charley. Like I said, we don't have a lot of facts. I'll have to attribute some of the stuff to people who I think are probably lying and some other to unidentified police. I'd modem it to you, but I have some film… It's skimpy too. You'll have to get somebody in to process it. There is no place over here would have it short of a week." I didn't point out that his next deadline wasn't until the next afternoon. I knew it would be counterproductive. I listened to him for another few minutes, said goodbye, and lay the phone back in its cradle.

Nature was calling urgently, but it was cold outside of the bed so I decided it was mind over matter and snuggled back under the covers. I hadn't decided if I would win or not when the phone rang again. I picked up and said, "Yes Charley, what is it now?"

The phone said, "Morning Ankus…. You ready for our little chat?"

"Morning Bernie. You got me at a definite disadvantage. I'm in bed and in terrible pain, and this phone won't reach the john. I'll be right back." I dropped the phone on the bed and could hear less than happy sounds issuing from it until I closed the bathroom door. Then, "Sorry about that. What time is it anyway?"

"It's nine thirty. You want me to come by there?"

"You at the station?"

"Home."

"We haven't even had a cup of coffee yet. I don't function too well without. Suppose we meet you at the station in an hour… Or I could buy you a doughnut at the bakery a little sooner."

"I better pass on that. I've already had breakfast and I don't really need that grease."

When we were ready to leave I turned on the computer and pulled up the file. After reading it through, I said, "You know, if we would change this one thing… Jimmy didn't say he killed the Finn, he just said he threw the maul at him. Change that like that and we could just print the file out and give it to Bernie." At her nod of assent, I said, "Ought to please him, and maybe he will give us a little information."

The scene at the bakery changes little. The same faces and the same topic as the day before. Everyone knew that Jimmy had been arrested, though it had only been since the middle of the night. The only dissent was on his guilt or innocence. Sherry listened as she sipped what she termed a decent cup of coffee for a change and asked, "How will we ever find a jury in this county that doesn't already have an opinion about this case?"

"I don't know about that, but I'd suggest another cinnamon roll if we weren't already late for our appointment. We better hustle on down to the cop shop before Bernie gets impatient and comes looking for us. Really start the tongues wagging if they came in here and busted us and dragged us out in cuffs."

We left the warmth and the pleasant aromas of the bakery and walked the half block to the police station in the cold drizzle. We found the door locked, with its sign saying "In case of emergency, call 911. All other calls Monday through Friday, 9 to 5," and listed a number I recognized as that of the city hall. We stood in the partial shelter of the doorway and watched the cars go hissing by. After about ten minutes I was getting cold and was about to suggest a return to the bakery when Bernie's little police car turned the corner and went behind the station.

He opened the door from inside and said, "Sorry... I didn't think you would get here so soon. You didn't sound too together on the phone."

Figuring to keep him on the defensive, I said, "Damn weather, we're half soaked. Why does anybody want to live in this miserable country?"

"Haven't you heard? This is paradise. There's heat in the back room. Why don't we go back there and sit down?"

In the back was a room with two desks, one facing the radio console, and the other the single cell, with the two chairs fighting for position in the space in between. The one detention cell looked like it would be crowded with two persons. I said, "When we left you last night we went home and put the little we knew and all we suspected into the computer. It really isn't all that much, but I ran you off a copy." He took the two pages and sat rubbing his neck behind his right ear while he read it through, twice, with only a few grunts.

He looked up and said, "You know we got a call to the Safehaven about an hour after you went home last night."

Sherry said, "That place... I wouldn't think you would be too surprised."

"No, we don't ever get called to that place. I think if somebody got shot in there they would haul the body out somewhere else and wait for us to find it. Anyway, we got called to break up a fight. As we walked in there were a couple punches exchanged… I think for our benefit because there wasn't any blood showing on any of the combatants.

Some glasses broken and a couple chairs dumped. Younger insisted we arrest them and he would prefer charges. We figured they just wanted to get into the South Bend Hilton. We brought them here and locked them up, and then never found time to transport them. Let them go about daylight, so we wouldn't have to feed them. I figure we were right because they got real pissed when we let them out."

We went over the printout with him, taking turns telling him all we had done since yesterday morning. He seemed pleased with the printout and to believe we were leveling. I took a chance and told him I had to write something for Charley by the afternoon, but hopefully would be following up on the story. I promised him anything I learned, and asked if he would let me in on the autopsy report when it came back. He made no promise, but I was sure I would get it, especially if I made him prominent in my story.

Sherry thanked him for helping protect Jimmy and we moved back to the bakery for a refill. Then I folded myself back into the Z and lay back watching her as she drove the fifty miles to South Bend, through the drizzle, to see her client.

CHAPTER EIGHT

At South Bend, Sherry eased up the hill to the Pacific County Courthouse, a local tourist attraction because of its hundred and fifty-year-old architecture. The few cars in the parking lot probably belonged to tourists here to admire its ornate rotunda. It has stairs curving up around either side from the entry, leading up to the cupola, with murals on all the inside walls, and the ceiling is colored glass, all depicting scenes from local history.

We walked down alongside the courthouse to a boxy concrete structure, hanging over the backside of the hill, where the tourists never go. It is mostly hidden from sight, as if to keep it from intruding on polite society, as its inmates are hidden where society doesn't have to acknowledge them. The unblinking eyes of two TV cameras mounted up on the side of the building announced our arrival to those inside.

Sherry punched a button under the grill of a speaker, in a blank wall, beside a blank steel door. The speaker said, "Visiting hours ain't until two," in a bored tinny female voice.

"S. J. Thompkins, Attorney, here to see my client, Jimmy Beasley."

This was met by a lengthy silence. Tired of waiting, her finger started again for the bell, and the speaker sputtered and then said, "OK, we found your name on the papers. Someone will be right out." I thought the person must be psychic until I remembered they had undoubtedly been watching our every move on their TV.

After another wait, with a clatter of its locking mechanism, the heavy door opened. The uniform inside was as tall as I, and would outweigh me by over fifty pounds. I'd always heard how bad jailhouse food was. Obviously at least the guards ate well. This one didn't believe in unnecessary effort, even to the use of unneeded words, he said only, "Follow me."

We followed: Down a hall, up a half flight of steps…down another short hall. He selected a large brass key from a ring hanging from his belt and opened another solid steel door, and finally got long winded. He said, "I'll bring him down," as he locked the door behind us.

I immediately felt claustrophobic. The walls were concrete with a steel door in each side of the room, and a long window that obviously didn't open onto the outside world. I figured it was probably a one-way mirror. The floor was concrete, with a steel table bolted to it. There were four chairs, two on each side of the table. Sherry slid into one of them. I attempted to move the other one toward hers and discovered they were also bolted to the floor. I then became aware of the TV camera. Next to the ceiling in the center of one wall, staring down the length of the table.

Again we waited. Sherry, knowing the system, sat making small talk. When I complained about the delay, she said, "Petty bureaucrats demonstrating their power. They probably don't have to bring him more than thirty feet. I try to not give them the satisfaction." She was interrupted by the second door, on the side of the room opposite from the one we entered by, clattering open. "Hello Jimmy… Come in and sit down." The door closed behind him with that metal on metal clang and the bolt snapped into its socket with finality.

Jimmy stood just inside, with his back against the door, and looked at us warily. Sherry stood and motioned him toward the chairs across the table, but he remained rooted. She finally crossed the room and took him by the elbow and led him to a chair. Then it hit me. He had never seen us in daylight. As Sherry came around the table, I stopped her and said softly, "He doesn't know who we are. It was dark out there last night and far as he knows he has never seen us before."

She turned and looked at him and said, "I'm sorry Jimmy... Don't you remember last night? You remember I told you Judge Harriman sent me to see you didn't get hurt? I told you I would get you a paper saying the truck is yours so nobody can take it."

His mouth said, "I remember," but his eyes said he wasn't sure, and wasn't sure she was really a friend as he sank warily to the edge of a seat across from her. He said nothing more.

In her best motherly tone, Sherry asked if they were treating him okay.

He said, "They put me in the women's jail." His tone seemed to infer he was insulted by it.

"That's good. I asked them to put you where those other guys couldn't be mean to you and they probably don't have any women in the jail right now so that was easiest."

"I got a TV."

Then it came to me. There hadn't been a TV in the Beasley's house. Probably out past where cable from Long Beach was available.

"That is nice. I just stopped by to make sure you were OK. I'll be back in tomorrow because we will see the judge then, what they call an arraignment..."

Jimmy interrupted with, "But I can't change the channels." Momentarily nonplused, she asked what he meant. "It's outside the bars where I can't reach it."

Promising to ask the guards about it she continued, "I still don't want you talking to anyone about hitting Suolo. That was the truth, what you told us about throwing the maul at him and running?" At his nod she asked, "Where did you get the maul?"

"It was there."

"There? What do you mean? Where was it exactly?"

"It was there... There by the bed."

She gave me a knowing look and said, "Jimmy, we are going to go now. The judge will see you some time tomorrow. I won't know the time until I call them tomorrow morning to see what time it is set. In the meantime, I don't want you telling them any of this. Do you understand?" At his nod she went over to the wall under the TV camera and pushed a button I hadn't even noticed and talked to the wall above it.

The wall answered back in the same female voice as before. "Okay, someone will be right up."

Preceded by the ominous rattle of the lock, the same overweight guard, even less loquacious than before, came to escort us out. Sherry asked about the TV. He said, "Jail policy." At her request for clarification he added, "It's in the hall… So nobody can mess with it. So nobody gets electrocuted and no smart lawyer sues us."

"Sorry Jimmy, guess you will have to put up with it. We will see you in the morning."

She was quiet for the first twenty miles as she stretched Washington's speed limits slightly. We then got behind a string of cars plodding along behind a huge motor home pulling a large boat. In the winding section of road it was ten miles before it was our turn to pass. She was champing at the bit. I said, "Relax and enjoy the scenery. It's Sunday. We don't have to be anywhere at any special time."

She answered, "Somebody set this up."

"What do you mean? These things run up and down the highway like this all of the time."

"No. I mean the maul. How many people keep their maul in the bedroom?" At my head shake she asked, "How many people who are falling down drunk take their maul to bed with them?"

"Pretty sharp. I guess I missed that one. Guess being in that steel box sort of shut my head off. Don't know how they handle it… The guards or the prisoners."

"I know… Don't think I will ever get over it totally. But some of the prisoners are more at home there than they are outside. Can't function without someone telling them what to do with every minute of their life. That's why some of them go back inside over and over. Spend more of their life inside than out."

"When we get back, maybe I should call Bernie and make sure they check the maul for prints."

"I'm sure they already have," she answered. "I'm not sure I want to draw their attention to it yet though." After a few more miles she asked, "Damn… Don't you ever get hungry? Let's go in to Long Beach. I'll even buy."

"I can handle that. I've got to get back before too long though. Take me a couple hours to put something together for Charley." We were making up some time on the straight stretch before town when the helicopter, with the big number eight on its side, came over. Channel eight, NBC TV News from Portland. I made the unnecessary observation, "It begins. You're going to get tired of seeing those guys in the next week."

When we pulled in to the curb by the police station, back in Long Beach, there was a young woman writing down the phone numbers from the door. A young guy with a camcorder on his shoulder was watching her. The camera had a big number six on its side. CBS Portland heard from. He turned it hopefully in our direction as we got out of the car, but lost interest when we ignored him and turned up the street toward the bakery.

"Vultures," Sherry said between tight teeth.

"You mean like me? They are just making a living. Wish I had their expense account so I could do it with as much style as they do."

Sherry led the way into the bakery. I passed up the opportunity to zing her about settling for a doughnut when she was buying. The bakery does put out a mean hero sandwich, one of which we split. After the noshing I called Bernie at home. When he picked up the phone I asked, "What you doing at home? All kinds of TV down here by your office wanting to make you famous."

"Ankus. I don't need it. Just refer them to the Sheriff or the county attorney. They run for election… I don't need any votes. What you got on your mind?"

"I'm getting ready to put my story together and there are a few things I need to make sure I have straight."

"Like what?"

"Like the cause of death. Anything new?"

"No, officially I won't know anything until probably Wednesday at least, but it's pretty obvious isn't it?"

"Now you're sounding like the DA. Okay. The supposed murder weapon… The maul I've heard mentioned. You found it at the scene?"

"You are not supposed to know about that, but yes we did."

"I'm sure you checked it for fingerprints?"

"You are right."

"Damn Bernie. You're not making this easy. I take it you found the kid's prints on it…. Anyone else's prints?"

"You didn't hear this from me, but yes we checked…. No, there were no other prints… It was wiped clean, very clean. One of the kid's hands up on the handle and the other down toward the head."

'Thanks Bernie, I probably won't use that today anyhow, but I will probably be able to quote the TV tonight after the DA finishes interviewing for the five o'clock news. Don't that strike you as odd, or is it an old Finnish custom? Get falling down drunk and wash your maul handle before you take it to bed."

"It occurred to me, but it's not exactly what the County Attorney wants to hear and it's not my case."

"Thanks Bernie. I'll remember to spell your name right." The click was final…. As usual, he didn't even say goodbye.

With a stop at her office to check her answering machine, we made the short trip to the Gull. I saw it before she even stopped. The paper waving from the middle of the front door. On closer inspection, it was a sheet of yellow lined tablet paper held in place with about a foot of silver duct tape. Tape like the guys at the fish canneries use to wrap their hands to keep the crabs from pinching so hard.

It was unsigned, but the grammar, or lack of same, and the message, a repeat of what we heard at the tavern last night, left little doubt as to the author. Thinking of saving it for Bernie, I carefully removed it and stuck it to the inside of the door. The smooth surface of the tape should supply a good set of prints. The contents were not as disturbing as the knowledge they knew the right door to hang it on.

We barely got inside; I had just turned the computer on…when the phone rang. I couldn't help but wonder if they had my phone number also, but it was Charley. He was his usual jolly self until I made him happy by telling him I would be over in a couple hours with tomorrow's front page, if I could get off the phone. I reminded him I would have some film and hung up and got to work.

It was slightly longer than the promised two hours. Sherry was asleep on the bed when I finished. After I got her awake I let her read it to see if I was messing up her case too bad. She questioned a couple of minor points, but in the end my journalistic integrity was held intact. It would go as written.

"I'm an hour late now. You want to ride along while I take it to Charley?"

"I'll drive you. That's forty miles... Probably about double what your clunk has left in it. Wouldn't want you to get stuck over there because I've got plans for you for later tonight. I don't have to be anyplace early tomorrow so I think I'll just stay here tonight."

"Best offer I've had all day."

Charley was cordial. I thought for a minute he was going to thank me, or maybe pat me on the back, or, heaven forbid, offer a bonus. But that was beyond him. He wiped the half smile off his face, and as we left he said, "I'll probably send a man over tomorrow to do the follow up." But I figured the story would most likely be mine as long as I could keep it going.

We stopped at a local watering hole with it's smattering of sleepy customers for a couple of drinks and a little familiarity in a dark corner of the dance floor before making the trip back across the bridge. The mood lasted until we walked into my place. All of the lights were on. I was sure we hadn't left them that way because it was still daylight when we left. I looked around and couldn't find anything missing... Probably because I don't have anything worth taking. Then I saw it. The note was missing from the inside of the door.

CHAPTER NINE

Sherry's case of the jitters was immediately back. She backed into me and said, "I can't stand the thought of having those cretins going through my things. Why don't you ever lock your door?"

"If I had locked the door they would have broken in and we probably wouldn't be able to close it at all now." Pointing out they were my things that had been gone through would have been counterproductive at the moment. So would pointing out my door was so flimsy the lock wouldn't keep anyone out.

I moved across the room and turned on my computer. All of my files still seemed to be intact. I said, "Everything is OK here. Five will get you ten, old Cleave stuck that note on the door and went back to the tavern bragging about it and either Younger or the big old girl friend explained it could be used as evidence against him; I'd bet on the gal… Bet she came back here with him and saw to it he didn't touch anything else."

"You always stick up for her." I wrapped my arms around her and thought if I ignored it, it would go away. It didn't, she said, "I think you got something going for her."

"Be nice. You know you're my only indiscretion." I started to say there was more to the woman than met the eye, but thought maybe in light of her size, that would be difficult. I changed it to, "I just think she has a few more smarts than most of that crowd at that joint."

I disengaged myself and fixed a pair of drinks, with water that neither of us liked, as that was all I had. Sitting on the edge of the bed, I cuddled Sherry as she gradually calmed down. I became aware of the blank eye of my computer staring at us. After a while, I got up, fully intending to shut it off, but I couldn't resist popping up the list of what we knew that we had done earlier. I added the bit about the note and its retrieval and asked Sherry if she had anything to add. At her negative head shake I shut it off and returned to the bed.

Neither of us was much interested in the booze and I couldn't get her earlier mood to return. I finally suggested we could take a hot shower and go to bed. "You think I need a shower?" she asked.

"I think we both need a shower or something to get our mind off this mess for a while." I have a nice shower. A little black mold in the corners and in the folds of the curtain, but just right for two people. If they are very friendly, that is. Since I took out the little rubber doohickey that restricts the water flow, it will practically strip the skin off. Soaping each other down in the close confines always gets things going in my favorite direction. Tonight was no exception. We shared the only clean towel I had left, and were still half wet when we hit the bed and I turned off the light.

I decided it was a night to be gentle, so it was a long time before we went to sleep. I had a very good time and from all indications, Sherry did also.

She eventually turned over and pushed her back into me. Wrapped in my arms she was soon snoring softly. I wasn't so lucky. I was unable to shut off my head and lay looking at the wall that was faintly visible in the light from the street. I was finally drifting off when Sherry began jerking as if running from something, and making whining noises reminiscent of those of a puppy newly separated from his mother. I held her tighter in hopes of comforting without waking.

It earned me an elbow in the ribs and the whine became more like a feline growl as she reared up in the bed, ready to fight. I kept still, not sure if she were awake or dreaming. She stared wildly around the room and then mumbled something unintelligible and turned into my arms where she was almost immediately sound asleep. This time I soon joined her.

The jangle of the phone brought me fighting my way up through multiple layers of sleep. When I tried to raise up, my left arm, the one that had been under Sherry all night, collapsed under me. It was asleep from the shoulder down. I said, "Shit Charley, not again." It was either very early or another lousy weather day as the room was still half dark.

I finally extricated myself and snagged the phone from under the edge of the bed. I grunted into it, not too hospitable, and was met by silence. After a long minute, a voice said, "Sorry, wrong number," and the phone clicked and went silent.

Sherry asked, "Who was it?"

"Wrong number," as I dropped back onto the pillow, intent on returning to wherever I was when it rang.

She merely grunted and snuggled back against me, but only for a minute. She suddenly sat up and said, "How do you know? Maybe it was just someone checking to see if you are home so they can come and finish burglarizing the place. I saw it on TV. That's how they do it."

I thought, *another good reason for not having a TV*, and tried to go back to sleep, but Sherry was awake and wanting to talk. I hadn't realized how much last night's break-in had gotten to her. Any argument I advanced to the contrary, she still insisted that some of the tavern crowd were waiting for a chance to get back at us. I finally gave up and crawled out of bed. After a pit stop I shivered my way across to the kitchen end of the room and started a pot of coffee, the end of the supply until I went shopping.

When I slipped back into bed, Sherry yelped and said, "Damn! Why don't you ever turn on some heat? You're a damn sight colder than that drink you gave me last night." She flounced out of bed and I watched her backsides as she crossed the room to the bath.

By the time I watched her front side on the return trip, I became much warmer. I opened up the covers for her to crawl back in, but she said, "I'm going to check my machine," picked up the phone, and sat on the edge of the bed instead. She punched in some numbers and sat listening. I slipped a hand up under her arm to cup my favorite plaything and got my knuckles rapped by the receiver. She punched in her code and listened another few minutes, totally ignoring my attempt to gain sympathy for my wounded hand. "Lot of garbage on there," she finally said. "Several heavy breathers who didn't leave any message, but stayed on the line for quite a while after the tone. The one I was looking for, Jimmy's arraignment is set for one o'clock this afternoon."

Conceding the battle, I rolled out, and dug up a couple of cups, rinsed them out, and filled them with coffee. Carrying the cups back to the bed I smelled something burning. Sherry noticed it about the same time. I began sniffing my way around the room until I saw the wires around the little ceramic coils of the wall heater, that was probably older than I, were glowing. "Just the dust on the heater... Hasn't been on for a while." She had turned up the thermostat without my seeing her.

"No wonder it smells musty in here.... You never turn on the heat to dry it out."

"It's just my way of fighting the establishment. You want to joust with windmills sometime. You're a lawyer. Start a class action or something."

"What you talking about?"

"The local Public Utility District pisses me off. PUDs were formed to bring low cost power to the people, and are supposedly non-profit and owned by the people. Right?"

"Right."

"When I was in Longview, just a county away, the PUD had the lowest cost power of just about anyplace. Course they had natural gas they had to compete with that isn't available here. Power here is higher than it is across the river from a private, for-profit company. You know that broad made me put up almost a two hundred dollar deposit because I'm a renter and the former renter had high electric bills. I've never had to pay a deposit anywhere for anything."

"So you are going to freeze to death to prove her wrong?"

"You complained about the petty bureaucrats at the jail… Now I'm complaining about the petty bureaucrats here."

"You need a soap box?"

"Just depends on whose ox is getting gored. In South Bend, it was you complaining about them." Warming to the subject I asked, "Know why I moved down here from Long Beach?" Without waiting for an answer, I went on, "I refused to pay their damn poor tax."

"What do you mean? They don't have a poor tax."

"Ha! That's what that broad at city hall said when I questioned it. They call it a business license… A business license to rent an apartment. So much per unit for all rentals. She is naive enough to think the landlord pays it. Seemed shocked when I said they pass it on to the tenants so it becomes a tax on people too poor to own their own house. You're a renter in Long Beach, you should be griping."

"Goodness…. You are on one this morning. All of this because I got tired of looking at your goose bumps and turned on a little heat. You're a writer… Why don't you do something about it?"

"I tried. I wrote letters to the editor and nobody even paid any attention. Nobody answered my charges. The poor people who are most effected are too busy hustling to make a living to have time to do anything. You want soapbox? How about the people who can make more on welfare than they are paid to work in the local tourist business?"

"You're making me hungry. Why don't we go someplace and get some breakfast. I've got to get my lawyer clothes, and I need to get to South Bend to do some paper work before we see the judge… You are going with me aren't you?'

"I haven't heard anything from Charley so I don't know. He may send somebody or he may plan to just pick it up from the wire service. Yeah… I haven't had any better offers… Besides I can refresh my memory. Haven't seen you in clothes lately." I was talking to her back as she headed for the bathroom. It is a nice back and when I heard the sound of the shower I thought to join her, but found the door was locked. When she came out she was fully dressed.

I took my turn and as we were getting ready to leave I remembered the heat. It was all the way up to the top. Not being too smart I asked, "Don't you know, it gets warm just as quick if you turn it to seventy-five instead of all the way up and you don't have to worry about burning the place down if you go out and forget it?"

"You sound just like my father," she threw over her shoulder as she swept out the door.

I thought of complimenting her father's good sense, but fortunately my good sense stopped me in time.

About a mile up the road toward Long Beach there is a little roadside cafe that looks more like a fireworks stand. It is painted in garish colors, has two picnic tables with umbrellas out front for the few days each year when the sun shines, and a large hand-painted sign on an A frame at the edge of the street, that is intended to look like it is changed daily. It says, "Today Only, Fish and Chips, All you can eat, $5.95, after 5 PM." It is changed about every three months when the rain fades it to illegible. We have tried the fish and it is good, but today it was a lot short of five. They also do a good job on breakfast, if you are very hungry and don't worry too much about presentation.

To prove she meant it when she said she was hungry, Sherry whipped into one of the five parking spaces, leaving only four empty. The inside was not much of an improvement over the exterior. Two tiny tables and about five stools at the counter. The décor is modern clutter. The coffee was plentiful and much better than mine. Only because they use a can in less than a month, I'm sure. We each ingested a large slab of ham and a couple eggs, with a huge serving of refried potatoes accompanied by baking powder biscuits and jam. We lingered over third cups and talked about what little we had unearthed to this point. We ate so much neither of us wanted to move, and as we didn't have any place we needed to be right away, we didn't.

I finally suggested we stop at The Seaview Market, about a quarter mile up the highway, to pick up a can of coffee and some light bulbs. Sherry said, "And soap, and milk, and how about some food? Hell, you could spend a hundred dollars in there and still not have anything in your place to eat."

"How can you think of food after this?" I pointed to the empty plates on the table as I got to my feet. I stopped at the register on the way out where the waitress/cook fumbled around for our check and finally rang it up without when she couldn't find one. When we left we were still the only customers.

My mind was numbed with the caloric overload but by the time we reached the market I managed to come up with a reason for not overdoing the shopping bit. I said, "We can't buy a bunch of stuff if we are going to South Bend. It'll all spoil in the car before we get back."

"It's only five minutes to your place. We can run it down after I change. Grab a cart, I'll help you."

So I pushed and she began throwing. By the time we reached the end of the first aisle I could see I had a problem. We had more in the cart than I ever buy in one trip and there were about four or five more aisles to go. Stuff I could picture growing green hairy mushrooms in my refrigerator, as I would never think to look there for food.

I turned the corner and started up between the cereal and the dog food where I figured I could make up some time and came face to face with the big gal from the Safehaven Tavern. I didn't see Cleave anywhere so I figured now was my chance to ask her the questions I wanted, as I had told Sherry.

But I drew a blank, all I could come up with was, "Ah... Er... Hello. How are you doing this morning?"

I could hear Sherry snicker behind me.

CHAPTER TEN

She was as startled as I. Standing face to face with her for the first time, I realized she was not as big as she had looked in the tavern. She was several inches shorter than I, maybe even an inch short of six feet, but on wider she had me. She didn't look any the worse for wear after the long weekend at the tavern. Maybe she had graduated from amateur. Apparently doing some light shopping as she had a basket in her cue stick hand instead of pushing a cart.

It was Sherry who broke the impasse by saying, "Hi… I'm Sherry. I think we owe you thanks for the other night. I suspect it could have become a lot nastier."

I could see the woman was further shaken because it wasn't what she expected to hear. Taking my cue, I said, "Yeah, thanks. We never did hear your name. What do we call you?"

"Desiree," she said in a surprisingly soft voice. "Desiree Bennett," she added with a curve of her lip, as if she were used to people laughing. But then who would dare?

"Pretty name," from Sherry. "You work at the fish plant?" At her nod, "What do you do there?"

"Filleter."

"Yeah. Gee they still top dog?" She even had me convinced she meant it. At the girl's shrug she went on, "I worked a couple of summers there when I was in high school. I always used to envy the filleters... They made twice as much money as anyone else.... But I was always afraid of those knives, so damn sharp."

"We have to keep them sharp. If we didn't, we wouldn't make as much money and actually we would be more likely to cut ourselves."

I decided to jump in and said, "We don't understand what happened at the tavern the other night. The guys had been out hunting Jimmy and bugging the Beasleys so we stopped in to tell Melannie he had been locked up. You know... sort of head off any more vigilante action before someone got hurt. Next thing we knew, the whole place was on us."

"She didn't say that."

Sherry took back the lead with, "We didn't know what to think.... That was spooky. What did she say?"

"I don't know exactly... Something about you were there to start trouble. You being Jimmy's lawyer and all. You were there to point the finger at someone else and get Jimmy off. And she didn't think it was right to get him off after he had killed her husband."

"The police aren't sure he actually did it. As his attorney I am just trying to find out all I can of what happened. The police aren't even sure how he was killed yet. They locked Jimmy up to keep him or somebody else from getting hurt, while they sort it out. How many people knew about the bottle of straight alcohol they kept in the back room?"

Desiree had begun to relax, then her face went to undecided as she thought about Jimmy not doing the killing. At the question she went defensive, and said, "Bottle, what bottle?" Then we could see the expression change as her mind sifted through it. She said, "That's how they did it... We always wondered... Suolo could sit there all day drinking beer and just be mellow. Drunk yes, but still able to shoot pool or talk... Then all of a sudden, in just a couple beers he would be totaled. He would pass out or close, and they would send him home in a cab."

Sherry asked, "How about Melannie? She didn't seem to be too torn up at the loss of a husband… at least not so much she couldn't work?"

"I think she had more going with Younger than she did with that ugly Finn. Actually, I don't think Melannie thinks much about anybody but Melannie."

I tossed in, "How about that other barmaid… What was her name? Whose side is she on?"

"You must mean Helen. Helen Jefferys. No, she has no use for Melannie. Rumor has it she was sleeping with Younger until Melannie showed up and aced her out."

With a shudder, Sherry said, "Jesus… I don't see how anybody could crawl in bed with him… The guy's a slug."

"Ma'am, you obviously don't understand tavern people. He owns the joint. That's all that counts…. But I agree with you, he is a creep."

I took a chance with, "How about Cleave? You've obviously got a lot more smarts than him. I'd think you could do better."

"Yeah… Look at me. I don't get too many offers. Besides, he is good to me mostly. He is working today. Doesn't miss too much work. He only drinks on his weekends, usually."

I drew a half smile when I said, "I don't know… Sherry has been accusing me of having something going for you because I stuck up for you." Then I asked, "The note on the door… Cleave?" After a hesitation she nodded slightly. "And you came with him to get it back?" Another uncertain nod.

"Younger said you could use it to get him jailed."

"I don't know of any law against sticking a note on a door, but thanks for not messing up my stuff. I don't have much but some of it is hard to replace."

"Cleave wanted to mess with your computer, but neither of us even knew how to turn it on. I convinced him you would know who it was because of the note if he broke anything."

"That's sort of how I had it figured. Nice talking to you, Desiree, we have to run."

Sherry said, "Yes…nice… Be good to get this all straightened out so everybody can be friends."

We moved up the aisle, but Sherry had lost her enthusiasm. She threw in an occasional item, but I was beginning to think I might get out without taking out a bank loan at the check stand. As we rounded the second corner I spotted Desiree approaching the register with nothing much in her basket, and a half rack of generic beer in the other hand.

We checked out and headed up through Long Beach. Sherry ran into her office, a small white shake building with yellow trim around the windows. It began life as a cabin back when motels consisted of a string of cabins, but now it had gone condo and her and the bank own the tiny building and the postage stamp piece of ground under it. I waited while she went inside for about five minutes then we went a couple blocks east to the newer apartment complex where she lives when she is dressed.

I offered to accompany her while she changed, but she said, "No… Don't bother. It will be quicker if I go alone."

I knew from the tone that I had offended her, but I hadn't a clue as to how. "Do I detect a slight chill? What did I do to put the burr in your bra?"

"You didn't have to tell her I was jealous of her. That big…."

"We got her to talking. We got most of what we wanted to hear. I thought we did good."

"I'll think about it. I'll be back in ten minutes." So I sat, and she wasn't. It was closer to a half hour. I was half asleep when she slid in and hit the starter. She said, "My hair was a mess. I had to do something with it." She came out looking good in her lawyer clothes, smart and efficient, but not nearly so soft and cuddly as when she went in.

We stopped at my place and lugged the groceries inside. I made a mental note to do my shopping next time on a day when I had less help. I stuffed the cold things into the ancient little refrigerator that was only meant to hold a tray of ice cubes and a couple of bottles of mixer in its first life.

There was little talking during the hour's ride to South Bend. This time we joined the ever-present tourists and entered the doors under the carved sign that said Pacific County Courthouse, with a Roman numeral designating the year of its birth. I never could figure out those numbers. I still found the murals, pictures of pioneers engaged in the now almost extinct logging and fishing industries, gracing the walls of the upper floors and the colored glass dome with the sunlight showing through it, always able to slow my steps. I wondered idly as usual if someone had spent months on his back as he created the ceiling mural, as in the Sistine Chapel.

We climbed the wide stairway to the second floor and entered a small courtroom. The same one where a group of tree huggers met their ultimate degradation a couple years back. They ran afoul of the law in their defense of the Spotted Owl and its old growth tree habitat and were brought before the judge in this room constructed almost entirely of lumber cut from these same old growth Douglas Fir trees. In front of a judge who probably put himself through law school by working summers in the logging industry.

Sherry disappeared through a side door to pick up her paper work from the court clerk and arrange for Jimmy to be brought up early so she could brief him. I took a seat and started composing a description of the place for the story I hoped to sell. I knew the arraignment itself would only take about ten minutes and Charley would expect at least a couple thousand words.

When she returned, Sherry took a seat at the left table of two at the front of the courtroom. I moved up and sat in the front row behind her and leaned over the rail between us. She began reading the sheaf of documents. Calmly and unemotionally she said, "Asshole," and continued to read. At my prodding, she looked up as if she wasn't aware I was there and said, "Damned Prosecutor thinks this is going to help him get reelected. He's calling for willful and premeditated murder. That would be easy to beat and he knows it so he has listed every level down to manslaughter. He can blame the jury when he can't hang the kid."

With my pen poised over my notebook I asked, "Is that for publication?"

She surprised me by saying, "Let me think about that for a few minutes. Maybe so." The side door opened and the talkative deputy from the jail escorted Jimmy in, with his hands cuffed behind his back. Sherry motioned him to the seat beside her and asked that the cuffs be removed.

"Can't ma'am." Then before Sherry could argue, he added, "Policy."

"He can't sit like that. Least you can do is put them in front so he can sit in a chair." Without wasting further words, but obviously not approving, he loosened one cuff long enough to pull Jimmy's hands in front where he reapplied it. He then took a seat next to me, directly behind Jimmy in the front row. Sherry said, "I want to confer with my client in private, would you mind moving back a few rows?"

It was obvious that he did mind, but he said nothing as he grunted to his feet and moved back to stand directly in front of the door.

Sherry began with small talk. Jimmy sat, skinny body stiffly erect, a worried look in his eyes, and his manacled hands in his lap. When she asked if he was still being treated right, he said, "They moved me."

Concerned, she asked if he was in with other prisoners and he said, "I don't have a TV no more." She never did get an answer to her question.

Very carefully Sherry explained that they were here only to decide if he would have to stand trial. "The Prosecuting Attorney will read the charges… What they are saying you did…. Then they will ask you how you plead. That means did you do it. I want you to just say not guilty."

"But I did it."

"They are saying you thought about it before you went to the trailer and then went there to kill him. That's not what you did. You went there to talk and threw the maul at him when he wouldn't answer you. That's bad, but not what they are saying. I need you say not guilty… Nothing else…. Understand?"

"Yes ma'am."

I looked around the courtroom. There were only a half dozen people, none of whom I recognized. The Prosecuting Attorney, Jerome Easley, a medium height, stocky man in his mid-forties, with thinning red hair and self-important carriage, entered from the same door that Sherry had used. He was followed by an assistant who was about the same height, but was if anything thinner than Jimmy, carrying a stack of papers. Jerome stopped at Sherry's table to drop a few words, delivered in a tone too low for me to hear. She colored slightly and stuck out her hand to which he gave a perfunctory shake and then turned on his heel and joined his Man Friday who had staked out a space on the second table.

As if pre-choreographed, as soon as he sat down the Clerk of the Court stepped from a door behind the bench and began his spiel, most of which I ignored, until he concluded with, "Judge Joseph G. Harriman, Presiding. All Rise."

Ah... good for our side, I thought, *we have a friendly Judge,* and tried to catch Sherry's eye when she stood, but she had on her best poker face and didn't move a muscle.

Judges are always imposing. It has to be the robe. You probably wouldn't remember this man if you met him on the street. Slight, with thin receding gray hair and glasses perched on a sharp nose. There was no doubt who was in charge in the court room when he briskly took his seat and picked up the gavel. He rapped twice and said, "Will the clerk please read the particulars?" Again I ignored most of what the clerk was saying as I tried to get an impression of the judge down on paper.

The prosecutor interrupted by saying, "Your honor, there are people from two TV stations out in the corridor. They want permission to film the proceedings."

The Judge said, "We can do very well without them. This is no circus. Is the defense ready?" At Sherry's "Yes, Your Honor," he turned and asked, "The prosecution?" and got the same answer. He then asked, "Will the prosecutor read the charges?"

Sherry said, "Excuse me your honor, that won't be necessary. I have them and the prosecutor has done his usual efficient job of charging my client with everything but spitting on the sidewalk. We would be here all day."

"The sarcasm is not necessary Ms Thompkins," but I was sure I caught the flicker of a smile. "Is the defendant ready to enter a plea?"

"Yes Your Honor." And after a pause she added, "The defense pleads not guilty."

The Judge looked at Jimmy, and after a perceptible pause, said, "Very well. As to the matter of bail?"

The prosecutor was on his feet immediately and said, "Your Honor. This is a capital case. The defendant is charged with first- degree murder and hid out for days until one of our deputies was able to apprehend him. We think he should be held without bail."

Sherry watched him with a pained expression until he was finished. She then said, "Your Honor, as I said, the prosecutor has covered all the bases, but they don't have a case. They don't even have a cause of death at this time. My client wasn't apprehended, I talked him into surrendering to the deputy because I believed his life was in danger. And that was only about twenty-four hours after the supposed murder. Nevertheless, we are not asking for his release at this time. We think his life is still in danger.... We have information there was an attempt to harm him even after he was in jail. We ask only for an order that he be segregated from the other prisoners until such time as we can prove his innocence."

Judge Harriman turned to the prosecutor and asked if he had any objections. The man, caught unawares, shook his head and said, "No, Your Honor." The judge then called, "Deputy," and motioned the man forward. He asked, "Did you hear that?" At the man's hesitant "No, Your Honor," he added, "I hereby remand Mr. Beasley to your custody. You are to see that he is placed in a separate cell. Furthermore you will inform your superiors that he will be so segregated until he comes up for trial."

I was surprised she didn't ask the judge to have a TV put in his cell, but Sherry just said, "Thank you your honor." I looked at my watch. The whole thing had taken eleven minutes.

CHAPTER ELEVEN

We were packing up to leave before I became aware of the eight or ten people who had slipped in and taken seats toward the rear of the courtroom. As soon as the deputy escorted Jimmy out the rear door and the judge disappeared into his office, totally ignoring me they descended on Sherry. Each one was trying to get his question in and voice levels escalated. For me it brought back memories of our experience at the Safehaven Tavern, except these people all seemed to be armed with microphones.

I could hear snatches of: "How can you plead him innocent?"

"Are you going to plead insanity?"

" Is it true he bashed in the man's head with a splitting maul?"

Suddenly we were bathed in a very bright light. I turned to see four TV cameras, with lights atop, charging down the aisle and jousting for position. Their presence was explained when I caught sight of the bailiff, with a smirk on his face as he propped the doors open. I wondered if the prosecutor had put him up to it. The jail deputy helped by taking his time as he led Jimmy out of the rear door, slowly enough for the deputy to get his fifteen seconds on the air.

I also wondered if Sherry had some of the same thoughts as she stood, case files in hand, and waited with surprising patience until they finally ran down and quieted. She then said, "You heard what I told the judge. I pleaded my client not guilty because he is not guilty of the things the state alleges. All they have is some circumstantial evidence pointing to him. They don't even have a cause of death. Without a cause of death it is impossible to say who did it.

"My client is in jail because I thought he would be safe there. I recommended he surrender to the sheriff because I felt he would be safer in jail. There were people out there with rifles and shotguns who were pursuing him through the woods and trying to kill him because they figured with him gone, the police would not look any further. Some of these same people, deliberately tried to get themselves thrown into jail after he turned himself in, and we can only assume it was to get to Jimmy."

She turned her back on them and began packing her papers into her briefcase. The clamor began again. She held up her hand and the noise subsided slightly. She added, "Mr. Easley, the prosecutor, is the one who arranged for you to get in. I'm sure he will be happy to furnish you with all of the lurid details of what he thinks may have happened."

Surprisingly the crowd parted as she walked toward them and she pushed through between two cameras and continued toward the rear door. One of the cameras followed her up the aisle. As I edged through behind her I could see by the camera angle that his interest was well below the shoulders. I paused long enough to say, "Nice, huh? Shooting this for the Christmas party?" He didn't comment, except by blushing, but he turned and joined the others as they pressed in toward the prosecutor.

I caught Sherry in the hall and as we started down the steps I said, "Damn, Counselor... you do good work."

She turned with a slightly less confident look on her face and answered, "I hope you're right. I don't like to try my cases in the media, but I had to try to predict what Easley was going to tell them and hope I raised some doubts."

Outside she slid under the wheel of the Z car and slumped in her seat. I could see the last few minutes had taken a lot out of her. I slipped the miniature recorder out of my pocket and began to rewind the tape. When it hit the stop I pushed the play button. After about ten seconds she turned slowly and with a look of disbelief she said, "Oh Shit!"

Thinking she had forgotten something I innocently asked, "What? You forget something?"

"Did you have that thing going all through the hearing?"

Thinking I had done good, I answered in the affirmative.

She said, "You fool.… You know, if the judge had noticed, you would probably be keeping Jimmy company right now. Didn't you hear him say no to having the TV and Radio people?"

"But I'm not…"

"Shit… Don't give me but.… He knew you were with me. He would probably have thrown both of us in the can for contempt."

"Sorry… Thought you knew. I tape most everything. Never was worth a damn at taking notes. I can't write and listen at the same time. Hell, I have trouble walking and chewing gum at the same time. I've got what's her name… The bartender…at that other tavern. The night at the Safehaven. Our talk with Bernie…"

"That's not legal. You can't tape people without telling them."

"If I tell them, they won't talk. I just use it to be sure I get my quotes straight."

"Do me a favor. Don't use it again in Judge Harriman's courtroom. At least when you are there with me." She leaned back in the seat with her eyes closed and rubbed the back of her neck for a long minute, then leaned forward and turned the key.

As she wound her way down the hill to Highway 101, I volunteered, "I've been listening to my stomach grumble for the past hour. Pull in to the Boondocks Restaurant down there on the right and I'll buy us a meal in a real restaurant." Without comment, she pulled into the parking lot. I escorted her into the place and asked the waitress for seats overlooking the docks.

The place was nearly deserted. They were as short of tourists in South Bend as they were in the beach towns.

Still almost not talking, Sherry idly watched a fishing boat that was showing its years, as it chugged slowly downriver toward the Pacific. When the waitress dropped the menus I asked her to bring us a glass of white wine, hoping to relax Sherry a bit.

She asked, "One glass?"

Exasperated, I said, "Yeah. With two straws. She's driving." Sherry snickered, so I relented and said, "Sorry. Two glasses." After the waitress had moved away I added, "Welcome back."

After a brief blank look, as if the gears had suddenly meshed, she said, "Sorry, I get this way sometimes. I'm never sure I am a good enough attorney and most of my clients are only looking at a little jail time. I'm sure Easley is going to ask for the death penalty. No chance he will ever get it, but this is still the big time for this little old country girl."

"You trounced him soundly back there just now."

"Don't kid yourself, Easley is a pompous ass, but he is pretty sharp. And he has some damn smart people working for him."

Glancing up from the menu and seeing the waitress returning I asked, "Then how about some brain food?"

"You better not be talking about liver."

As the girl set the wines on the table, in my most diplomatic manner, I said, "Save you a trip. Why don't you bring us two large bowls of your clam chowder?" As she started to turn away I added, "And a pair of your best Salmon Steaks." This apparently strained her memory as she stopped and pulled a pad from the folds of her apron, wrote it all down, and asked what we would have to drink. At my, "Coffee, maybe later," she gave up and headed for the kitchen.

"Your idea of a light lunch?"

"I have a feeling this may be dinner too. When we get back I have to get something on paper for Charley and get it over to him. Probably should check in with Bernie and see if he has learned anything new." And as an after thought, "I need to do some checking. See how much that Finn was really worth…and also make a few calls to check out the insurance angle." Sherry agreed that she needed to get back to her office to take care of some business, but offered to check out the

86

insurance part.

The food was delicious as it usually is at the Boondocks, and we were both in a better mood. Sherry looked down her nose at what she considered an exorbitant tip, but said nothing. I had kidded her in the past about having to carry a calculator so I could figure the fifteen percent that she figured to be a proper tip. Ten percent I could handle; just move the decimal, but fifteen went beyond the threshold into higher math. Besides, I needed to salve my guilty conscience for my earlier faux pas.

She was her usual self on the trip back, even to the normal lead foot. I kept expecting a state patrol car to appear out of a side road, but nothing happened. When she pulled in to the Gull parking lot I asked, "Want to come in for a… while?"

"No thanks. We both got work we need to do and I have a feeling that's not what you have in mind."

"Will I see you later this evening?"

"I don't think so. I better sleep in my own bed for a change. Those little old ladies next door are going to think I've moved out…. Or worse they will be sending the cops out to find me as a missing person. Figure some old letch has kidnapped me."

I stood in the parking lot and watched the little car as it made the right turn on a red, without the required stop, and headed up toward Long Beach. Thinking… arguing with myself… *she's quite a lady. A guy could do a lot worse. But without the challenge, how long would it be this way? I tried it once and permanent just don't seem to work for me. Besides, she would probably turn me down. I'm old enough to be her father. Well almost.*

These thoughts have gone through my head a thousand times in the past year or so. And questions I'd likely never have the answer to because they were questions I would probably never get around to asking.

I went inside. Immediately I sensed something amiss. I had the feeling someone had been in the place. I could feel the hair on my arms tickle. I looked around, opening every door… That is the bathroom door and the two cupboard and one refrigerator doors. Nothing seemed out of place. I thought, *Sherry has me doing it too… it's all in my head.*

I turned on my computer and dialed the police station while I waited. A feminine voice answered and I asked for Bernie. I idly ran through the files while I waited for him to come on the line. Everything appeared to be in order. He came on with, "Yeah… What's up Ankus?" Not friendly. Not unfriendly. Just business.

I decided to be likewise. "Been to South Bend for the arraignment. Wondered if I missed anything?"

"Like I said before, I won't hear anything until they finish the autopsy. Ain't my case anymore anyhow," I told him about the note on the door and the later visit. He said, "You need to do something about that lock."

"Hell… You know I'd have to replace the whole door and probably the wall it hangs in before I got any more security." I told him about our grocery store visit with Desiree and my impressions, then offered that I got the feeling the whole thing was over.

"Don't bet too much on it." Then sounding vaguely familiar, "Was I you I'd watch my backside. That bunch had one brain between them they would know better, but if they get the idea it will get them in good with Younger to do you in they could get ugly."

I thanked him and cradled the phone. Resisting the strong urge to turn and look behind me I went to work on my story. An hour and a half later I had managed to stretch it to eight pages double-spaced, close to the two thousand words I knew Charley would expect.

Since I had no art, I got Charley on the phone and told him to expect it by modem. He grumbled about the lack of pictures but accepted my explanation that they didn't allow any cameras in the courtroom, after voicing his opinions on bureaucrats abridging the freedom of the press and walking all over their rights.

I went through the file we had in the computer, listing the little we knew and added a few lines. I sat and listened to the tape from the courtroom. It didn't add anything new. I was beginning to feel alone. I looked at the clock and it was almost four-thirty. I could walk over to the Bay View Café and watch the news at five. They always had the TV on.

Once in a while it would be nice to have a TV, but mostly it was a waste of time. And cable was damned expensive for what little I would watch. Besides that's how I got acquainted with she of the big boobs at the café. I started out the door and then stopped and looked back at the computer. Cursing myself for a fool I went back and turned it on. While it booted I dug out a couple of floppies, formatted them, and proceeded to copy all of the files on my hard disc. It took a while, as it is one of those things I dislike, and I had not done it in a long time. I dug a brown paper bag out of the trash and stuffed the floppies in it.

It was now five minutes to five. Feeling rather foolish, I took the bag, crumpled it up, and shoved it under the seat of the car, after checking first to see that I wasn't being watched.

When I walked in the restaurant door, the blonde was behind the counter, cramming napkins into a holder. I asked her if it were true that there was a special school that all waitresses had to attend where they learned to put in so many napkins it was impossible to get them out. She started to look affronted, but looked at the door behind me and saw that I was alone and her half frown turned to a smile.

I sat down at the end of the counter where the TV was mounted on the wall and asked for a cup of coffee. "No wonder you are so skinny. You need more than coffee." When I explained we had eaten in South Bend, she insisted I had to try the apple pie. I know it's un-American, but I don't particularly like apple pie. But the news was starting and I knew the arraignment would be the lead story so I agreed, to cut off the conversation.

I laid the recorder on the counter so I could review it at leisure. The interview with Sherry came up. She had been so short and succinct they were running it verbatim. "Oh… That's that lady lawyer you were in here with the other night." I turned and there was a huge piece of pie in front of me with a mountain of ice cream on top. At my complaint she added, "You need it. Give me a chance, I'd put some meat on those bones." With a smirk, "You wouldn't get fat, I'd see to that."

The TV was introducing the Prosecutor. He came across as a pompous ass. He had obviously done as Sherry had predicted, and at great length. They had chopped it into little bits to fit the time frame and made him sound even worse. It was good I had deployed the recorder as the blonde wanted to talk. At the moment I was the only customer so I was elected.

I ate most of the ice cream and a little of the pie while we carried on a conversation. Mostly hers and mostly suggestive. Two older couples came in and continued through to the small back room. Acting not particularly pleased she picked up a stack of menus and followed. I thought of bolting, but she was back before I had my wallet out. Frowning she picked up the coffee pot and returned to the back. Feeling a little less than brave I put enough money on the counter to pay at least double what I owed. I picked up my recorder, looked at the cup of coffee, but decided not to chance it, and ducked out the door.

Back at the Gull I opened the new can, put on a pot, and fired up the computer. I had a feeling it would be a while before I was interested in sleep so maybe I could get a few more words on the novel I had been working on for the two years since the printing of my last one. My mind wasn't really on it so as usual of late, I didn't accomplish much.

One of the reasons I elected to live at the beach in spite of the lack of cultural events and the abundance of rain was being able to not lock everything. Now, in the back of my mind, I was mulling over how to do just that. I was reminded of Sherry's jitters of last night. And Bernie's warning didn't help. I was feeling less than confident. I knew the locks on these flimsy doors were useless, and if the lock held, the whole wall would come down easily. Cramming a chair under the doorknob occurred to me, but the door opens out so that wouldn't work.

I finally talked myself out of the notion that anyone would be out to get me. But I didn't get much writing done.

CHAPTER TWELVE

I sat at the keyboard and pecked out an occasional word. It wasn't coming easy. My characters just weren't talking to me that night. Actually they had been mute for several nights. I suspect they tend to avoid Sherry, or avoid me when she is around. It was, shut my eyes and screw up my face, hit a few keys, shake my head in disgust, and hit the backspace and watch the little blinking light gobble up the offending letters one at a time. Sort of like the old Pac-man games.

The place was too quiet. It always is the first night or so after Sherry goes home. I got up and turned on the radio. The set cost less than ten bucks at the local thrift shop so I am limited to one local AM station with oldies and a couple western stations across the river. I don't usually care which. I am mostly just looking for noise to fill some of the empty corners, so the room doesn't feel so big and vacant. I chose the local station tonight, because I didn't think I needed to listen to any sad stories. It spewed out Christmas music, one song after another. In between they kept reminding me there were only twenty some more shopping days before my least favorite holiday.

Then I remembered why I usually don't eat apple pie. I'm not sure whether it's the cinnamon or the apples, or maybe it's the combination. Something there always fights back. The rumbling in my stomach let me know this night was not going to be any different. I gave up after adding less than a page. One I would probably eliminate the next time I sat down at the computer.

I flipped up the file I had titled Jimmy and studied it in hopes there was something to give me an angle for another story. Something I could sell to Charley. Nothing clicked, so I listened to the tape of the arraignment. Sherry still sounded good and Easley still sounded pompous, but neither made another news story.

By this time I had guzzled half the pot of coffee and was beginning to slosh so I checked through the stuff we had picked up at the grocery. This was a weakness I couldn't usually indulge as there was normally nothing edible in my cupboards. I finally settled for a handful of snack crackers and a slice of cheese, and stretched out on the bed with another cup of coffee and a book.

The bed was also big and lonesome and the book not very interesting. So on the theory the book would put me to sleep, I undressed and climbed between the covers to read. The book was still not interesting enough to keep my mind from wandering over the last few days and I kept coming back to the warning from Bernie. For the life of me, I could think of no good reason for anyone to threaten me. It would accomplish nothing, but I had to admit to myself, when that tavern crowd gets all boozed up they would probably think differently... Or maybe they aren't capable of thinking. I was sure there had been people from the tavern at the hearing and there probably wasn't much else being talked about at the place that evening.

I finally drifted off, but the coffee caught up so I had to make the trip. It was almost eleven when I turned the light off again, after rechecking the door lock. I eventually went back to sleep, but it wasn't very soon.

I must have finally been sleeping soundly. I fought my way up through layers of sleep with the feeling I had lain down in the center of a monster truck rally. The sounds of un-muffled engines were accompanied by the hoarse yells of an indeterminate number of riders and the repeated honking of horns. Lights pierced the thin curtains and crisscrossed the ceiling, and the squeal of tires followed the roar of the motors.

I slid out of bed and made a stooping dash for the wall along side the window. I cautiously raised the corner of the curtain, but the window was so steamed I couldn't see through it. I stood and pondered. If I wipe the window off will they be able to see it and know I'm watching? But they know I'm in here anyway or they wouldn't be out there. Something fairly substantial hit the outside of the wall where I was standing, with a solid thunk. I was colder than hell standing there with no clothes.

Another something sounding like a brick hit the door. I got pissed and reached up and wiped the window with the corner of the curtain. I almost immediately decided it hadn't been such a great idea. I didn't really like what I was seeing.

My field of view was limited, but at least three large pickups, jacked up so high the driver should have an oxygen mask, were cavorting in the parking lot. Careening through the circular drive in the darkness, they looked like grotesque, overgrown mantises. With headlights on high beam, and driving lights mounted above the cab blazing, they were making a tight circle through the motel parking lot and the street in front. The riders in the back were mere shadows except when the lights of another truck would sweep across them.

Another missile hit the wall. They had to be drunk. The windows, while not very big, were still big enough to make an easy target from about twenty feet, even from a moving truck. Or maybe they were just out to scare me... I confess they were successful. Or maybe it was just that no one had nerve enough to deliberately break a window.

The lights in the owner's unit and most of the other apartments came on. The drivers ignored them and continued to circle. I heard a crash and the tinkle of broken glass from the bathroom. Someone must finally be getting the range or maybe the nerve. It seemed as if it had been going on forever, but I was sure it was less than ten minutes.

Suddenly, voices were yelling, "Cops," and with a loud honking of its horn, one of the trucks broke away leaving a cloud of evil smelling smoke from its squealing tires as it raced away down the street toward the docks and incidentally the Safehaven tavern.

Thinking, *There goes my sleep,* I shrugged into my jeans and one shoe. Before I could find the other there was a banging on the door. Not sure of what I would find, I hobbled over and opened it a crack. The owner of my elegant abode, a normally friendly man named Bob Nichols, obviously not very happy tonight, was standing in front of it. I opened it further and could see other heads emerging from other doors. Smelly blue smoke from the exhausts was still hanging lazily in the air. By the aroma, at least one of the trucks had been a diesel.

"This is a quiet place! I won't put up with this sort of behavior. I called the cops on those friends of yours."

Catching sight of a brick in front of the door, obviously the object that struck it earlier, I picked it up and asked, "This look like friends? I don't know who they were. Thanks for calling the cops."

"What do you mean, you don't know who they were? They knew you. They weren't throwing things at anyone else."

That wasn't what I wanted to hear. I already knew I was undoubtedly the target of their attentions, but this sort of brought it home. "I think I know who they are… Sort of. I think they are some guys from a tavern who object to a story I wrote for the paper…"

"I don't care… I won't put up with…"

He stopped in mid-sentence when a police car with red and blues flashing, wheeled into the parking lot and nailed us with his headlights. Nichols headed toward it. Before he reached it a second car pulled in and spotlighted my neighbors who were collecting a couple doors from mine. Their backup, a county sheriff's car, unable to pull into the already filled lot, double-parked in the street in front.

The flashing lights from the three cars, bouncing off the motel windows as well as being multiplied by the windows of the darkened storefronts across the street, had an eerie, surreal effect. It was almost disorienting. The owner was talking to the driver of the first car and pointing to me and to the side of the building as well as gesturing to illustrate the actions of the departed trucks. When the car door opened

I half expected to see Bernie.

The cop motioned for the owner to stay by the car and moved over to where I was shivering in the doorway. When he got closer I recognized him as the man who was with Bernie at the tavern a couple of nights previously. He asked, "You OK?"

"Yeah… No blood leaking out… Just freezing to death. Come in while I grab a shirt."

"Bernie said we should keep an eye out. Another hour and we would all have been home. You recognize any of them?"

"No, not really. I'm sure it was some of the Safehaven bunch, but with all of those bright lights I couldn't see anyone. Just trying to scare me off I reckon. I don't think they meant me any real harm."

"Don't bet on it."

Nichols, tired of being ignored, pushed his way through the partially open door. "Look at this. Nobody will get any sleep. This has to be your fault, it never happened before."

"I asked you to wait by the car. I need to question all of the witnesses separately."

"It's cold out there."

Hoping to placate the man I said, "He is right. It's cold as hell," as I closed the door behind him. "I don't think any of us saw enough to do you any good." I still had the brick in my hand. "This is one of the bricks they threw. Sorry I grabbed it. Probably can't find any prints other than mine on it now. Should be another one somewhere outside the window.

"Oh… There's another one somewhere in here," as I headed for the bath. When I opened the door and saw the glass strewn all over the floor, I knew I didn't want to go any farther. I still had only one shoe.

With a strangled sound, Nichols pushed in and said, "The window… It's broken…. Who's going to pay for this? I won't stand for…"

The officer interrupted his tirade with, "Mr. Nichols, that is evidence of a crime that you are walking on. I'm afraid I am going to have to ask you to wait outside the room while I find the object that was thrown."

Foreseeing myself walking down the road with my belongings on my back, I said, "Come on Bob, let's sit down in the other room and let the officer do his thing. I'll pay for the window… Maybe I can charge it off as expenses on the story."

Somewhat mollified he sat on the edge of a chair. He said, "Can't have this sort of thing… People are entitled to their sleep." But his tone was less strident.

The officer came back into the room. He held up a plastic baggy containing a large rusty bolt. I made it about three-quarter of an inch by eight inches. He said, "This could hurt if it hit you. Between this and the bricks… You still think they didn't want to hurt you?"

There was a rap on the door and it was pulled open. Sergeant Malahovsky shouldered his way through it. I hadn't seen him out of his car before except in the dark out at the Beasley place and never realized just how big he was. Apparently he was driving the sheriff's car parked in the street. He nodded a greeting to me and turned to the other officer. "I got another call. You got everything under control here?"

"Yeah… I'll be OK. Thanks for coming. Tell Carl he can go with you if you need him for backup."

"Thanks Sergeant. I owe you a thanks for the other night also." At his questioning look I added, "Thanks for sending Bernie to The Safehaven Tavern. We could have got our heads banged good in a few more minutes."

With a grin he said, "You need to pick a better class of joint to do your drinking." And he pushed out through the door.

I said, "Bernie used that line already." Then I offered, "I can put on a pot if anyone is interested in a cup of coffee."

"Not me, I'm sloshing now," from the police officer.

"You got to be crazy… Never get any sleep…. I never drink coffee after dinner," from Nichols.

We all followed the sergeant outside. The cop picked up the second brick with another baggy and brought it back into the light of the door. "Probably won't get anything off this one either. Bricks like this all around down by the docks where they tore down a couple of old buildings years ago. So much moss and dirt on them prints won't show."

"You done with me?" Nichols asked. "I would like to get a few hours of sleep. I'm going to have to get this mess cleaned up come daylight." Since the cop had picked up the only brick outside and I had agreed to clean up the inside, I wasn't sure what mess he referred to, but I wasn't dumb enough to say so.

The cop said, "Go ahead Mr. Nichols. I'm done here, I'll be leaving shortly."

I watched him as the officer walked up toward the office and stopped to talk with the other tenants. From the arm motions I could tell what they were talking about. He came back my way, and I said, "Guess I owe you another thank you. You always seem to be rescuing me. I never did get your name?"

"Robinson, John Robinson."

"Thanks John Robinson. Hope I don't require your services again tonight. Or any other night for that matter." He headed for his car and I headed for my bed in hopes of getting warm.

It was when I started to remove my one shoe that I remembered. I needed to do something about the window. Both parts. The glass on the floor and the lack of glass in the wall. By the time I located my other shoe, had the glass swept up, and a towel tacked over the hole, it was after four. I crawled between the covers, sure I would still be awake and shivering come daylight.

CHAPTER THIRTEEN

The ringing phone woke me. *This is beginning to be a habit. Who the hell could be calling at this hour? Not Charley again I hope,* I thought.

It wouldn't stop, so I finally located it under the bed and pulled the handset back under the covers. It was talking non-stop, but it wasn't Charley. Not unless he'd had an operation. When I got myself comfortable, I put it to my ear. The voice became Sherry and she was talking a mile a minute. I was able to gather she had heard about last night's shivaree. When I found an opening, I said, "Hello," innocently, as if I had just picked it up.

"What do you mean, hello? Jesus you piss me off sometimes. I've been talking to you for five minutes and all you can say is 'Hello.'"

"Isn't that the way everybody does it? The phone rings, so I pick up the phone and say hello, then you say hello, and everybody knows there is someone on each end of the wire before they start talking. That way no one gets pissed off because they got their feelings hurt by the other guy not hearing what they said."

After a long pause, I could feel her counting to ten, she said, "I saw

Bernie when I stopped by the bakery this morning. He told me about those guys throwing bricks through your windows last night."

"Bolt."

"What do you mean bolts?"

"Bolt actually. Singular. They threw a bolt through the bathroom window. The bricks only hit the outside wall."

"You're trying your damnedest…. He said you could have been hurt."

"What time is it anyway? You talk like it's noon."

"It almost is, it's ten-thirty. You mean you are still in bed?"

"It was four o'clock before I got the mess cleaned up and the broken window covered, and I was half frozen so it took a while…."

"I wouldn't think you would be able to sleep after what happened."

"Yeah, that took a while also. You hear anything new about the Beasley thing?"

"No. There won't be any more until we see the results of the autopsy. That won't be until at least late tomorrow probably. I've got an insurance guy I know making a few inquiries about the guy's insurance. Sort of hinted we suspected fraud. But that will take a day or so also."

"I thought lawyers were above stretching the truth…. As I said before, we'll make a reporter out of you yet. Damn. I'd like to come up with something for Charley. If I don't and he uses the wire services to keep the story alive, I may never get it back."

"Why do papers feel it is necessary to keep a story alive?"

"I guess to sell papers. People buy papers to keep up on the gory details. They buy papers and writers who provide the gory stories get to eat. That's the American way."

"You're trying to change the subject. What happened last night anyway?"

"I suppose Younger and or the grieving widow got the boys all pumped up. About closing time three or four pickup loads of them spread a layer of rubber on the parking lot in front. Some brave soul pitched a couple of bricks against the front wall then someone with a bit better aim slung a bolt through the bathroom window. It was rather intimidating at the time, but in retrospect, not so much."

"Not so much… You could have been hurt, Bernie said."

"Bernie wasn't here. Damn. That reminds me…. Who does glass? I told Nichols I would get the window fixed… After he threatened to evict me." That brought out the lawyer in her and we spent the next ten minutes on why he couldn't do that. I finally got off the phone, blaming the need on the call of nature, which wasn't too far wrong. I studied on it and thought about cooking a pot to wake up my brain, but didn't have the ambition. The only thing I could come up with was to call Bernie again, but I had been using our friendship too much, he hadn't been too friendly the last time. I finally dialed the station.

Officer John Robinson answered. On the theory, a little flattery will get you a news story, I again thanked him for the night before and then commented on his not getting much sleep. He remained friendly and we chatted, but I was not getting anything useful until he mentioned the local all-night restaurant and said, "We drove by after we left your place. Three jacked-up four-wheel rigs were in the lot so we stopped for a coffee. No way to prove they were the ones, but they sure shut up when we went in. We made a production of looking them over and writing down the names of the ones we knew, just to make them feel better."

"Younger wasn't there whipping up the troops?"

"No, didn't see him…. Actually, we did a walk through at the tavern earlier last night and he wasn't there either. That other barmaid, Helen I think, was behind the bar."

A bit more flattery and I hung up. Interesting, but still no story. I brought my Jimmy file up to date. It was still very short. In desperation I finally dialed Charley in hopes he might have a lead I could follow.

His opening line was, "You seen any TV lately?" When I admitted I didn't own one, he said, "You keep telling me there is nothing going on. They always seem to be able to find enough to run a story."

"Hell Charley, you know how they operate. Check the facts and you may ruin a good story. They figure the viewers will forget the story by tomorrow and since they don't have it written down nobody will be able to point out their errors."

"They got that Beasley kid as some kind of dimwit monster with blood up to his elbows, running around the county killing people until the cops apprehended him."

"I'm sure the prosecutor's office has been leaking stuff. Just wait until Sherry gets the kid acquitted. The TV will just ignore it because there will be no record of what they said before and an acquittal won't be a story worthy of their air. You put it down on paper and it will be around to haunt you, even if you do have to read it hanging in strips in the local outhouses."

"You trying to piss me off or something?"

"Must be a problem with my phone. Sherry asked the same thing.... Reason I called... Who do you know would be able to tell us how much the departed was worth? His boat is supposed to be worth a quarter mil, but a lot of these fishermen are in hock for their next twenty years catch."

"Want me to do your leg work for you now? Hmmm... Just might be able. OK. I'll make a couple of calls and call you back. Maybe I ought to save some money and write it also."

"Thanks Charley... I'll be waiting." While I waited, I sat and studied the Jimmy file, but it lit no sparks. I began to think maybe fiction was better. I could think of several ways the story could go with a bit of imagination.

Thinking, *Charley didn't waste any time* when the phone rang, I snatched it up. It said, "John said you called looking for me."

"Bernie... I was expecting somebody else," as my head shifted gears.

"Heard you had some sort of loud party at your house last night." Without waiting for my witty rejoinder he asked, "What's on your mind?"

"You know me. Just trying to scare up something new to make a story."

"Just turn on your TV. They don't seem to have a problem finding a story."

"Have you been talking to Charley? He jabbed me with the same question. I can't do fiction. Charley insists I check my facts."

"If you could identify those jerks from last night we could arrest them. Intimidating the press or some such. That would sell a few papers.

Maybe if you keep pushing them someone can write the story of your demise."

"Wish you hadn't told Sherry. She's shaky enough. Oh… We are working on how much the Finn was worth and how much insurance he had. I'll let you know what we get."

"Told you it's not my case anymore. You get your head split, that would be mine… 'Less you let them kill you; and then the county prosecutor would probably take over again."

"Pleasant thought. Relying on Easley that is. He would probably declare it a suicide, even if I had six bullet holes in my back."

"Got to go… The other phone…. See you."

I sat and looked at the blinking cursor. Four calls and not a line to add. I was wracking my brain for a way to go, but no bells rang and no flash bulbs went off. Maybe I should stick to fiction… But then I hadn't been scoring too high in that category lately either. The phone rang again. Maybe the fifth time would be a winner.

"Why don't you get call waiting? I tried you earlier, but your line was busy." Charley hadn't wasted any time. "The fisherman was doing all right. Off the record of course…. The boat was free and clear, as was his house." To my remark, denigrating the house, Charley added, "The house is not much, but it is on a couple of acres of property that overlooks the river… It's probably worth another couple of hundred thousand dollars…. He also had a bank account that stayed in the middle five figures."

"That's a lot of motive…. But I'm not sure how it makes a story. Especially if it's off the record."

"You been in this business longer than that. That just means you didn't get it from me. Attribute it to some informed source." When I didn't respond right away he said, "Maybe you should get out of this racket. Maybe you should go cozy up to the new widow. Hear she is a looker… Sounds like now she is a rich looker."

"Maybe you have something there." The bell hadn't really rung, just sort of tinkled. "Wonder if the widow knows how rich she is? She sure as hell won't have any need for Younger and his crummy tavern. I need to figure some way of getting to her, by herself, away from

Younger and the tavern. Thanks Charley," as I hung up on him for a change.

I sat and thought about it as I entered the latest into the computer, but I knew there was no way she would meet with me. Not alone. Going to the Safehaven was out of the question. I picked up the phone and dialed Sherry. I spent five minutes filling her in on what I had learned. " Rich bitch," was her only comment.

I very carefully went back over it, finishing with, "She probably doesn't have any idea… She could buy half a dozen Safehavens. She don't need Younger any more. I was hoping you could come up with an excuse to see her alone. You know, stir the pot a bit."

"Shit!! I remember the last time you stirred the pot. Almost got us killed."

"That's why we need to get her away from the Tavern. Can't you call her? Nobody will think anything of another woman calling… lay some of that lawyer talk on her. She has all that money coming… She should talk to an attorney… You know, make sure she don't sign any papers, even hint she could join her husband if she isn't careful."

"Jeeze…you're getting real devious. But it might work. Get them separated and hopefully fighting each other. Let me think about it for a while. I'll get back to you."

I sat and stared at the computer screen. It wasn't going to be easy. I finally began: 'The citizens of the small town of Oceanside are on edge. Usually the killings here are simple. Somebody gets mad at somebody else and does him in, as often as not in front of a dozen witnesses. This time it is different. A man was killed, alone and in his own bedroom. Some know the killer is locked up. Others disagree and think the real killer is still running loose. There is talk of booze and drugs, and also about large sums of money. Informed sources report the deceased was worth in the neighborhood of half a million dollars, possibly with insurance above that.'

Then I sat and watched the cursor blink again. I had no idea where the story was going from there. My stomach reminded me. It was after noon and I hadn't even had a cup of coffee. I thought again of brewing a pot, but decided it was too much trouble. I saved what little I had written, shut off the computer, and walked across to the Bay View Cafe. It was one of those rare days in winter when the air was sparkling clear. Cold, even in the bright sunlight, and the ships entering the river were plainly visible over the water, even though they were over five miles away. The sun must have brought out the tourists as the restaurant was busy.

Just goes to show, as a local would say; the bad weather is what makes this place livable. Keeps the tourists at home. All Doris had time for was a smile with the cup of coffee she placed in front of me when I sat down at the counter. No time for small talk.... Another plus, come to think.

Feeling somewhat better after my second cup and a hot butter-horn drenched with butter, that I stuck with despite the hassle from Doris over how I eat, or don't eat, take your pick, I wandered back to my castle. I heard the phone ringing from half a block away, but thought to hell with it, if I run for it the damn thing will just quit as I go through the door. It didn't. It was Sherry.

After settling the whys, as in why did I take so long to answer, to my satisfaction if not hers, she laid out the plan she had hatched. "I got Melannie at the tavern. I explained that you had been digging out information for a story and had found out that she would be receiving quite a bit of money."

I didn't say it, but thought, thanks a lot, if Melannie uses that with those goons at the tavern, it will prove I am asking all those questions I have been warned about asking.

"I told her she should be careful about who she talked to and shouldn't sign any papers until she saw a lawyer. She agreed to stop here at my office at one this afternoon. I told her you would be here to tell her what it was you found out." On the surface it sounded all right.

But what if she talked to Younger about it? I'm sure he would not be all that happy about our meddling and if he put his mind to it he could arrange for a lot more interesting entertainment for us than that of last night.

CHAPTER FOURTEEN

Sherry was right about my car. I was late getting to her office because the damn thing didn't want to start. It's a tired old Chevy four door, fourteen, or is it fifteen? years old. I know it isn't long for this world, but it's a man size car. I hate the thought of spending much time folded up in one of those little plastic boxes they are peddling as cars today.

It finally started in a cloud of smoke, after I zapped the carburetor with the spray can of something that smells of ether or some other foul smelling chemical. The can says, "Guaranteed to start your car in the coldest weather." A mechanic friend says, "Guaranteed to kill your motor in any kind of weather." It's only necessary when I don't start the beast for several days, especially in cold weather, which makes it Sherry's fault since she is the one insisting I shouldn't drive it.

I watched the blue cloud of smoke drift lazily across the parking lot while I waited for the motor to reach the point where I could trust her on the street. I thought, that's good. Not the smoke, but the fact that it was moving slowly. Days at the beach when the wind doesn't blow are to be cherished, especially when it is the front end of December. The smoke, that's something else. My mechanic friend... Actually friend is stretching it a bit… It's friend for a price…had explained about blue and black smoke. Neither is good, but one is worse. Trouble is I could never remember which.

We made the three miles to Long Beach. The heater had just reached the point where my feet were beginning to thaw. I parked and walked across the street to the little white-shingled building with yellow trim. I felt late. I had no idea what Melannie would be driving, but Long Beach streets are not very crowded midweek in winter and I could see no car I figured to be hers. The only car within a block was Sherry's Z.

I had my pad and my tape recorder in my hand as I reached for the door handle. Remembering Sherry's reaction to the recorder yesterday, I stopped and pushed the sound activation button and then the on button, and then put it in my shirt pocket. With my jacket closed, I hoped it would escape everyone's notice.

Compact was the word that came to mind. The room I entered was maybe ten by sixteen feet. She had set it up as a reception area with a desk, file drawers, and a computer for her secretary, even though she couldn't afford the secretary as yet. Her answering machine was the single attendant when she was out of her office. The door to the second office was open and I heard no voices so poked my head in and said, "Sorry I'm late. Hope I didn't miss the show." The second room was a duplicate of the first in size and layout; desk on the right and chairs straight ahead. The only deviation was the Lilliputian rest room sandwiched into one corner.

She looked up from across the desk. I'm not sure if it was for show or for real, but she had a large law book open in front of her. "You're late, but Melannie is later. Maybe she decided not to attend."

"You did use the word money?"

"Several times, and she did sound interested. Maybe she is having trouble getting away from Younger."

"If he found out, you know he would nix the idea. I figure she has more smarts than that." Seeing the glint begin in Sherry's eye, I didn't finish the thought. Instead I casually wandered out into the front room to stare out the window at the deserted street. I was about to suggest we go someplace for lunch when the door opened and Melannie slipped in. All I could think of was, "I didn't see you drive up."

All smiles this afternoon she answered, "I parked behind the bank and walked across. Everyone knows my car and I didn't want anyone to know I was coming here."

I ushered her across to the inner sanctum and Sherry stood and pushed out a hand and a smile in greeting. I seated her in a chair facing the desk. The only other chair was beside hers and I wanted to be able to see her face, so I hung one cheek on the corner of the desk. Sherry opened with, "You know I am representing Jimmy Beasley. We are investigating everyone who has any connection to this mess." A shadow slid across Melannie's smile, but it was fleeting, and she forced the smile to return. Except her eyes. They weren't smiling.

Sherry tossed it to me with, "Tom was checking Suolo's financial situation and learned a few things you may find of interest."

When I spoke, I had her full attention. Probably the use of the word financial. "First there is his boat. It is worth in the neighborhood of a quarter million dollars. Other than maybe some fuel bills or moorage fees it is free and clear." That eliminated any shadow on her smile. "We found one bank account. Don't know if he had any others, but this one has about fifty thousand dollars in it." The smile widened. "Then there is his house."

"That junky old trailer isn't worth much."

"You are right there. The trailer is probably only worth eight or ten thousand. But the land is something else. He had a couple of acres… Cut a few trees back of the trailer and you got prime view property. Probably worth about as much as the boat. You appear to be in line for all of it. Maybe as much as half a million. All together you are a wealthy young lady." It took a minute. She kept the smile but I could see the brain working as she added the figures. It was also obvious most of this was news to her.

"That is unless they decide you had some part in his death," from Sherry. Melannie lifted in her chair and started to protest, but was quick enough to realize we were not the proper forum. She sank back and rearranged her smile and waited as if she knew there was another shoe. Sherry added, "We have some people checking on any insurance on him." She didn't say that he did indeed carry an insurance policy. "Any recent policies are going to require a lot of explanation before the companies will pay off on them."

I tossed in, "With all of that you won't need Younger. You can buy your own joint. Hell you can buy two or three of them if you want… Nice places even."

She sat with that smile playing on her face for so long I began to wonder if she was still with us. I was about to interrupt when she gushed a very sibilant, "Yesss." At my puzzled look, she added, "Like that fish place up town… I heard it is for sale… I heard it got locked up because that lesbian who owned it got caught doing drugs. That could be a real nice place."

Sherry pounced. "So how about your husband's death? We know Younger sent the kid up to his place. And we know Suolo was so drunk he was helpless. We know about the straight alcohol that got him that way." Melannie was slow coming back from dreamland. Her smile disappeared and she sat up in her chair. Sherry added, "You know you won't get any of the money if you were part of it. How much of it was Younger and how much did you help with?"

She was back with us, totally. Her eyes hardened and she said, "I don't know anything about it. If somebody from the tavern had something to do with my husband's death, I didn't know anything about it."

Sherry bored in with, "We have witnesses that involve Younger. You can bet he isn't going to take all the blame, and if he implicates you… There goes all that beautiful money."

Melannie was irate. As she bounced out of her chair and headed toward the door, she gritted, "I don't have to listen to this crap."

Before she reached the door, Sherry hit her with, "If Younger is accused, you think he will defend you?" As the girl half paused, she said, "I wouldn't sign any papers with him without the advice of a lawyer. With all that money you are of value to Younger, but if he can get control of the money he won't need you. Then if you disappear, you could get all the blame." I hoped Melannie wasn't listening too close at that point. If she got blamed, there wouldn't be any money, so he would have to protect her from being blamed in either event.

Melannie started to say something in return, but thought better of it and slammed out of the front door.

"Hey lady…. You can really get rough when you want."

"It was your idea. You said we should stir the pot. No use screwing around. She will either tell Younger and get him to do something or she will split from him and he won't take kindly to that… Not with all that money. Get them fighting each other and somebody is apt to make a mistake… Let something slip."

"Yeah… Somebody will be throwing rocks through your windows next. Maybe you should stay with me for a while."

"You never quit trying do you?"

"You would be unhappy if I did." I walked out to the front room and looked at the sunshine washed street. I added, "We could walk up town in this beautiful weather and get some lunch. Maybe by that time Bernie will have the autopsy report."

"That's not due until tomorrow at the earliest," then Sherry added. "This is still only Tuesday."

"Jesus, it seems like two weeks since Charley woke us up Saturday morning. Anyway, if we would just drop in on him and tell him what we found out and what we just did, maybe he would return the favor and give us a look at the report when he does get it."

"I can get a copy of the report from the county. Discovery. They have to furnish one for the defense."

"But when? That might take a week or more. I could hang a story on it. It's getting tough finding anything to write about and Charley is getting impatient."

"Poor baby… I'm more interested in saving my client," as she hung out the, 'I'll be back in a little while' sign and closed the door behind us.

The walk was pleasant. The streets were still almost empty. We met a jacked up, older, black Chevy pickup at the first corner. They are plentiful on the peninsula and in the past I never paid them any attention.

Today I did. He slowed noticeably as we turned toward the crosswalk. I stopped and held Sherry on the curb, and waved him past. This abnormal act elicited a searching look from her, but she didn't say anything. I didn't know either, but I did ponder on it the rest of the way up the street. Who was it said, "A coward dies many deaths?" I don't know, but a guy could sure waste a lot of time ducking pickups in this town. He could also die a quick death if he stepped off the curb in front of the wrong truck. Every other citizen on the peninsula owns one of the things.

The bakery was as empty as the streets, at least of the local gossip mongers. A couple of the local business people were having lunch and spoke to Sherry. There were a few tourist types who probably came to the beach to storm watch and were disappointed because of the nice weather. The winter ocean can be spectacular, but when the wind dies off, it gets as quiet as the off-season town.

We sat in the front window and dawdled over our sandwich while we watched the street. The few tourists who were not enjoying the weather on the beach were doing so on the street. No one appeared to be in any hurry. I did notice several jacked up four-wheel drive trucks, including the black Chevy making its return trip. I told myself I was being silly. They are just trucks. But when the next one would appear I couldn't keep my eyes from following it and my head from wondering if it could be one of those from last night, as my muscles tightened up.

The booth seats in the bakery are made of plywood. People joke about it being softwood. But after the best part of an hour, my posterior was beginning to complain. I got little sympathy from Sherry when I complained. She said, "You need to put some meat on your bones. Maybe you should start hanging around the Bay View and let that big tit blond floozy fatten you up."

Ignoring the gibe, I suggested we relocate. "If we have all of this time to kill, I'm sure we could find a more comfortable accommodation at my place." The offer didn't even elicit an answer, but she did begin moving and we were soon out on the street.

When we passed the police station I tried the door. When it surprised me and opened, I entered and peeked around the corner. Bernie was at the desk, working over a stack of papers. He waved me in and said,

"Hello Ankus. What you doing today to endear yourself to the good people from the Safehaven?"

I explained what we had done. He frowned his displeasure as he listened. He said, "Jesus H Christ… Beg pardon Counselor…. You must be slow learners…. Won't you ever learn, those people can get downright ugly?"

Sherry said, "We just wanted to split them up or get them to fighting among themselves. I even warned Melannie to watch Younger to make sure he didn't put it all on her and do something to get rid of her."

"I'd think it would work better in reverse," he said. "If she can throw the blame on him and get someone to eliminate him…. That way she would still get the money. She gets blamed, there isn't any money."

"I got half way there after she left Sherry's office. I realized if he got her blamed there would be no money, but never thought about her doing him in."

"Did you also realize they could get together and decide you two were a threat to them. If they were responsible for the Finn's death, they could very well think that a couple more don't make any difference."

Sherry said, "Damn Bernie, you sure have a knack for putting things in a way to get a person's attention." As we started to leave, she turned to me and said, "The offer you made earlier is beginning to sound much better. Is it still open?"

Bernie gave her a "what was that look" and she said, "I stay at his place tonight. That way we will go out together."

Bernie said, "Funny. Ha, ha. I agree. You shouldn't be alone. But I'm not sure his place is that safe a place to hide out."

CHAPTER FIFTEEN

When we left the police station, Sherry had definitely taken Bernie's warning to heart. In the short walk back to her office she agreed, with no prodding on my part, to spend the next couple days with me. No baiting, no hassle, just, "Let me go by the office for a minute, then by my apartment long enough to pick up a few things, and I will follow you home." I did my part by keeping a straight face, but had to admit to myself, my good feelings were not all because of the mutual protection part of the arrangement.

After the visit to her office we were heading for her car when a four-wheel pickup with a loud muffler rumbled down the street. The whole thing was really starting to get to her. This time it was her that stopped and eyed it until it passed before she ventured out into the crossing.

I had only been in her place a few times. It represents her respectful side. Her Shangri-la as it were. She worries about her old maid neighbors and their opinions, and as I said before, she does her slumming at my place. But today she asked me to accompany her while she picked up a few things. Afterwards, she dropped me back at my car, waited while I coaxed it into life, and then followed me back to my place.

From the street, the Blue Gull looked peaceful in the weak winter sunlight. I hadn't paid much attention lately, but on reflection, it looked more abandoned than peaceful. It is blue-gray with blue trim that has not been freshened in a number of years, and the coastal weather is not kind to paint. Most of the windows were blank and staring, with no curtains in evidence. It's patrons had them pulled back full open. They were probably trying to capture the sun's meager heat and light to cut their electric bills in this place of little insulation, or perhaps they had nothing better to do than keep track of their noisier neighbors. I was sure Sherry's presence was duly recorded.

I needed to earn a couple of bucks so I sat down at the computer. Sherry curled up on the bed, giving my powers of concentration a test. I frequently sit with my eyes closed and compose my contribution to tomorrow's birdcage liner on the inside of my eyelids, but the vision of her lying there on the bed kept filling up the space.

I added a few comments about last night's visitation to the "what we knew" file, and started on our session today at Sherry's office. I read it off to Sherry and asked if she had anything to add. Receiving no answer, I turned to check. She was sleeping quietly.

I pecked out a note to Charley, complaining about the lack of much to write about, and then hammered out a couple thousand words, half about anonymous sources reporting the Finn being well off, and the rest just a rehash of previous stories. I wasn't too happy with it and was sure Charley would feel the same, but I was fairly confident he would use it. I tagged on a promise of more tomorrow, hopefully after we saw the autopsy report.

Sherry was snoring softly. I debated waking her to run the story by her, but didn't have the heart. I put on a pot of coffee; sort of hoping the smell would bring her around, thusly relieving my conscience. It didn't work, so I sipped while I read the story through again and found nothing I figured she would object to. Still needed something, but damn if I knew how to fix it so I hit the necessary buttons and watched as it slid into the phone wire. I'll never be totally comfortable with watching something I have sweat over for hours, disappear in seconds, even when I know I have saved a copy. As usual, I picked up the phone and wasted a call across the river.

Charley's secretary, Beverly, said, "Yes Tom. Just knew you would call. I was about to put it in front of his majesty. You want to talk to him?"

"No I think I will give him time to get used to it."

"You know Tom, like I've said before, your computer will tell you if it isn't able to reach us."

"Guess I'm old fashioned. Can't get used to a machine that talks to another machine and then talks back to me. Guess I just like the sound of a human voice."

"OK, It's your nickel. Probably be talking to you tomorrow."

I flipped over to my latest book effort and dinked around with it for a while. At the end of an hour, it had become dark outside, I had consumed three cups of coffee, and I had added two short paragraphs. And I wasn't very proud of them. I was just too aware of Sherry asleep on the bed, or at least that was the best excuse I could come up with.

Leaving the computer on I headed for the bathroom. Since I was already there, and hadn't been accomplishing too much anyway, I decided I might as well shower. It then seemed only logical that I should shave, in light of the evening I hoped was ahead. The robe, Sherry's gift, was hanging on the inside of the door so I put it on and went back into the other room.

Sherry was sitting in front of the computer, cuddling my coffee cup and reading my book effort. She had pulled the curtains behind her tightly closed, shutting out the budding night and its terrors. She asked, "Not great literature is it?"

"Thanks... I needed that. How you expect me to concentrate with you curled up on my bed? You looked positively edible."

"You've got a one-track mind. I see you found the robe." She turned back to the computer and asked, "Did you get Charley's story written?" When I pulled up the file, she read through it and said, "Really not much here either is there? When you going to send it to him?" When I told her I already had, she gave me a nasty look and said, "I thought we were in this together."

"I read it to you, but all you did was snore."

"I don't snore."

I switched to the "what we knew" file and asked if she wanted to add anything. When she declined, I remembered the recorder. I laid it on the table and turned it on.

She said, "That damn thing again. You're going to get us both in trouble with it one day. Why don't you take a memory course?" But she sat and listened to the repeat of the session in her office. The quality wasn't good, but most of it was understandable and she sat through it all without further comment. She turned back to the computer file and I leaned over and nuzzled her neck. She squirmed on the chair and after a while began to moan. After a few minutes she suddenly turned to me and opening my robe did nice, unmentionable, things to the body within.

It didn't take long for her to get my full attention. I said, "This would make a lot better sense in the bed."

She leaned back and looked up at me. I thought I could see shadows in those beautiful green eyes. Soberly she said, "I think you are probably right. Why don't you hold on to that idea long enough for me to shower?"

"Maybe you would like a little help?"

"I think you are right. It would make a lot better sense in the bed. Why don't you warm it up?" she said as she moved across the room.

Watching the neat figure cross the room, I debated whether I would accomplish anything by following. The question was answered when I heard the lock click after she closed the door. Resigning myself, I set a pot of coffee for morning and decided to lock the door. I had to ask myself why, this being something I never did. I was late. Sherry had already locked it. Probably at the same time as she closed the blinds. Feeling rather foolish I rested a kettle on a chair in such a position that it would fall onto the floor if someone should open the door during the night.

I turned off the lights and slipped between the covers to warm the bed as requested. It seemed like a long time later that Sherry joined me. She complained, "How come you had to run the water... about parboiled me." My apology was the last intelligible sounds from the bed for a long time.

I was drifting off to sleep when Sherry scared hell out of me by suddenly sitting up in bed. I assumed she had heard something outside. She said, "Damn it, I'm hungry. I don't know how you do it. We never did eat anything after that skimpy lunch."

"I thought we were going to live on love."

"Yeah… And bullshit makes the grass. I'm going to fix something. You haven't eaten all of those groceries we bought the other day have you?"

"Couple of slices of bread. Some crackers and cheese. I never remember the stuff is here."

She said, "No wonder you are so damn skinny," as she bounced out of bed. I lay there and was treated to the sight of her practicing her culinary talents, in the buff. I hadn't been hungry, but it wasn't long before the delicious smells had my stomach growling and was almost enough to distract me from my pleasant voyeuristic pastime.

At the sound of bacon sizzling, I had to comment, "Are you sure you aught to be doing that without clothes? Hate to have you damage anything important."

"Where do you keep the pancake turner?"

"Don't have one… I never cook pancakes."

Very patiently, "What do you use to cook eggs or even fried potatoes?"

"Mostly a knife… Or maybe a spoon. Usually they break and I end up making scrambled."

"I can't cook without…. Tomorrow we're going shopping."

"We just did that."

"Dennis Company," she said as she opened and closed cupboard doors. "Dennis Company, you need dishes…. Silverware…pans…. You need everything."

I could see bankruptcy ahead, but knew better than to contest her demands at the time. Maybe she would forget before tomorrow or after we ate at least. She placed two steaming plates and two cups of coffee on the table. So what if they didn't match. My theory is, if you don't have many dishes, there are never many dishes to wash.

The food was good. A guy could get used to this. With my stomach full, I was beginning to yawn. In a "doing my share" gesture, I gathered up the dishes and started to stack them in the sink.

"Let's do them."

"They'll keep until morning."

"By morning you will have to use a chisel to get those eggs off. You can wash, I'll wipe."

By the time we had the dishes all put away, I was covered with goose bumps from the cold and it was after one. I turned out the lights and we slipped into bed. With a contented sigh she turned her back to me and curled up and I wrapped myself around her. She didn't feel a bit cold in spite of having wandered around in the cold for the past hour or more.

She was soon sleeping quietly and I was well on the way to joining her when it dawned on me. It was almost closing time for the Safehaven Tavern and that is the time its patrons usually picked for their games. If Melannie went back and told Younger about her visit, he could be arranging some un-pleasantries for us. On the other hand, if she didn't tell him, she might be the one doing the same thing. I finally drifted off to a fitful sleep.

I woke to the smell of coffee. I reached for Sherry and found her side of the bed vacant. I raised my head and found her sitting at the table, in my robe, with a cup of coffee, reading one of my books. She had opened the blinds and uncomfortably bright sunlight was streaming across the room. The sharp rays brought out the chipped paint on the walls and cabinets and the shabbiness of my garage sale furniture. Shabby, but not sheik. It did little in general for the shoddy interior of the room. I watched Sherry for a minute, she always looked good in any light. I finally said, "Morning love."

With a start, she raised her head from the book and said, "I was beginning to think you would sleep all day." The clock above her head indicated nine-thirty. Add ten or fifteen minutes because I hadn't set it in a month or so and I rounded it off to almost ten. Obviously, we had no visitors during the night, but with my recent record, it was hard to believe there had been no phone calls by this late in the day.

I sat up and put my feet on the floor and Sherry brought me a cup of coffee. "A man could get used to this. Breakfast at midnight and coffee in bed. You looking for a permanent position?" All it earned me was a raised eyebrow, and I decided the matter might be better left unexplored for the moment.

We made small talk and decided to head up town for some breakfast, and took turns in the shower. It was coming up on noon and we were both dressed and about to leave when the phone rang. I made a face and said, "Charley." When I picked it up though it was Bernie, my friendly cop.

He said, "Morning Ankus. See you are still able to pick up the phone." I wasn't sure how to take that, but an answer obviously wasn't expected. He went on, "Somebody up in Portland must have made a mistake. Didn't realize the county had taken over the case. They faxed my a copy of the autopsy report."

I covered the phone and said, "Bernie. He has the autopsy report. Maybe I can get us a look at it." Back with Bernie I asked, "Any chance…"

He continued as if I hadn't interrupted, "Makes some interesting reading. Very interesting. The Counselor will like it I'm sure."

"Least you could do is read it to me."

"Haven't got the time. Tell you what. I'll make a copy of it for you. Very unofficial and you didn't get it from me. I have to come down that way anyway so I'll drop it by. Probably half hour or so."

In his usual fashion, he quit talking and the line went dead. No good-bye and no chance to ask for further information, so we sat and waited. I listened to my stomach growl and jointly we wondered what he found so significant.

Sherry's response was, "I'll still have to ask the county for an official copy. Otherwise it might be hard to explain where we got it. We probably shouldn't let anybody know we have it until I do."

"What you mean, don't let anybody know? I promised Charley a story as soon as I could get it." I could see the storm clouds gathering so I relented with, "OK… Wait until we see it. I can always quote a reliable source." But I knew Charley wouldn't be happy with that if he found out I had the report. We had used too many reliable and anonymous sources already. Oh well… Fight that battle when I couldn't avoid it.

CHAPTER SIXTEEN

We sat and waited. Every time a car passed, one of us would get up and look out the window. The half hour stretched to well over an hour. My stomach was getting louder.

Obviously something had changed Bernie's plans. At times I had considered a scanner on the theory it would alert me to possible stories. But always I talked myself out of it for the same reason I had no television. Too much noise. There would be no point in having one if it weren't on all of the time and the incessant babble would drive me up the walls. At the moment I was almost ready to change my mind.

Sherry said, "Why don't you get a scanner like everyone else on the peninsula? We would probably know where Bernie is instead of sitting here jumping at the sound, every time a car passes on the street."

"Lady, do you read minds? I was sitting here thinking about the same thing. Trouble is, to be effective you have to have the damn things on all of the time. They sit and chatter endlessly, and they are hard to understand if you don't either have them turned up loud or concentrate on what they are saying. Like you said, I got a single-track mind. I can't write and listen at the same time."

"That's not the single-track I am usually referring to." She was interrupted by the flash of red and blue on the ceiling. Bernie's way of letting us know he had finally arrived. The lights stopped when I opened the door. I looked up the row of windows. There was a face in every window but two. The owner's window was one of those inhabited.

I said, "Hi Bernie. Thanks for dropping by." I didn't say, are you trying to get me evicted? I just thought it.

"Sorry, it took a little longer than I figured. Little fender-bender north of town. Here's the report. Not sure why they sent it to me. Like I said earlier, it's not my case anymore. It was hanging from the machine when I got in this morning."

"Sherry said she couldn't use this, not until she gets an official copy from the county, but she is happy to get a look at it all the same."

"Interesting reading that, but as you will see, it isn't the final, just a preliminary."

"What do, you mean…?" I was cut off when Bernie leaned over to listen to his radio.

"Gotta go. Talk to you later," he called as he greased the little car out on to the street and accelerated up the highway toward Long Beach.

"Thanks Bernie," I said to myself. As I turned toward the door I unfolded the sheaf of papers. The paper was the thermal type. The pages that curl up and defy your every attempt to read them. With Sherry hovering, I finally spread them on the table, with silverware on the ends. The cover sheet, the thing that tells who sent what to whom, was absent. No way anyone could trace it back to Bernie.

The first page and a half were given to describing the deceased, his age and general condition, and all of the legal niceties. I skimmed through it quickly and went on to the meaty parts. Sherry read every word.

The phantom doctor spent the next half page, in a dry clinical manner, on the gruesome recitation of the weight and condition of each of the internal organs, and then went into the results of Jimmy's attack with the maul. My interpretation was, struck on the left temple just above the eye by a heavy semi-blunt instrument. Skin torn off almost to the ear. Depressed skull fracture. Severe concussion. All consistent with the maul discovered at the scene…. Then the first inconsistency: bleeding not as heavy as would be expected with a head wound of this magnitude.

Sherry caught up as I was reading this paragraph for the second time. "There," as she impaled the offending words with the nail of her long finger. "There. Lack of bleeding. That's enough to base a defense on."

I read it through again. "I don't see it. Sounds to me as if it proves Jimmy did it."

"There it says Suolo didn't bleed much. Head wounds always bleed a lot. Could mean he was already dead when he was hit. Maybe from the alcohol. All we need is to establish a doubt in the jury's mind. That alone would drop it at least to attempted."

"You are grasping. We better come up with more than that. Old Jerome baby would laugh you out of the courtroom."

The third page began with: The deceased had a blood alcohol level of point three nine. Then an explanation as if the author felt the locals might need further enlightenment. He spent half a page saying this would probably be a lethal dose for any but a confirmed alcoholic. He also noted the liver showed little damage consistent with prolonged and excessive alcohol abuse.

Sherry's finger got that one too. "See. That proves it. They fed him too much alcohol. It killed him. That is why he didn't bleed when the maul got him later."

"It just proves these Finns got a tough liver. Everybody knows he drank too much."

"But only on weekends. He worked on the boat all week."

"Are you sure he didn't take a supply with him on the boat?"

"That's something we better check out."

I wasn't sure we could get anybody to tell us the truth about this, as well liked as we were by the Safehaven bunch. The Finn undoubtedly had help on the boat, but did they drink with him at the tavern, or could we find someone who would be impartial? I said, "We should mention that to Bernie. We aren't too popular with the fishing crowd at present. Maybe he could get an answer."

The top of the third page produced the real zinger. A needle mark on the back of the right hand. Under the circumstances, it might have been missed if it hadn't been marked by dried blood in an area otherwise clear. Examination showed the angle of entry was such as to make self-administration difficult. No other needle marks on the body. A complete toxicology report would be forthcoming in three days to a week.

The report went on for most of the rest of the page with more legalities. Mostly the cover your own ass sort of stuff. But Sherry's finger became stuck on the paragraph above. After about three passes she asked, "What could this mean? We heard from several different people that Suolo was violently opposed to any kind of drugs. Who could have stuck a needle into him without getting him aroused and have him fight back?"

"I think, more to the point. The needle mark was in the right hand. Either the Finn was left-handed or worked awful hard to confuse the issue."

"Or it proves someone else shot him up."

"Obviously they were up to their usual. His blood alcohol proves that. Maybe they stuck it to him while they were putting him into the cab. That is if they sent him home in a cab. It's only about five minutes from the tavern to his place. I don't think that's long enough for most drugs to have much effect."

She said, "That depends on what and how much. We need answers to a lot of questions. Questions the cops should be asking, but aren't because they think Jimmy did it, and I think Easley at least prefers it to stay that way."

"We need to know if they sent him home in a cab. If we can find the cab driver, maybe we can find out when he went home. That is if the driver will talk to us. He probably gets enough fares out of the tavern to influence his answers. We know when Jimmy went to the trailer. Somebody else could have got there before him."

"Jimmy said he went there three times. Said Suolo wasn't home the first two times," she added. "Maybe somebody went there in between. Maybe Suolo was there when Jimmy went there, but didn't answer the door. Jimmy probably wouldn't have tried the door if it was shut."

Beginning to work together, I bounced it back with, "Yeah... you're right. He said he went there and Suolo wasn't home. To Jimmy that might just mean he didn't answer the door."

"We know he didn't answer the third time either, but Jimmy went in."

"Why then and not the first two times?"

She came back with, "The door was open…or partly. Or maybe the lights were on. If he went home early enough or drunk enough he probably wouldn't have turned them on."

"Ok, then person or persons paid him a visit. They accidentally or on purpose left the door open or the lights on so some one would find the body."

"On purpose would mean somebody who knew Jimmy was apt to be coming back. I suppose they could have seen him the first two times and figured he would be back."

I chipped in with, "Supposedly, Melannie and Younger were both working at the tavern that night. Friday night. Would probably be busy. That gives them a nice neat alibi, but nobody would miss either one of them if they slipped out for a few minutes. We've got to talk to that cabby. At least there is only one cab company on the peninsula. Usually only one driver during the off-season, who works with a cell phone, so he doesn't even need a dispatcher. But Friday night they would probably have more. Maybe we could get Bernie to lean on them."

"I'd rather we did it ourselves if we could. I'm never sure the cops will tell me everything. Why don't we call a cab and go for a short ride?"

"It might be better if we wait until the night shift is on. Besides, it's getting late and I need to put something together for Charley. Give me an hour and then you can read it over." I proceeded to walk a fine line. Since we didn't have the official autopsy report, I was able to quote an anonymous official to the effect that it had been determined there might be another cause of death, other than the maul, without giving too much detail. I again added a rehash of previous stories and showed it to Sherry.

She liked it, which forewarned me that Charley probably wouldn't. I dialed up the paper and sent it across the river. I didn't call this time, which may have been a mistake, because five minutes later the phone rang.

It was Charley. He opened with, "What kind of tap dance you trying to give me?" Without waiting for an answer he went on, "You haven't written anything new for the past two days." And then proceeded to cite as many of my other deficiencies as he could think of.

I very carefully explained that the official report would be several days, I mentally crossed my fingers, but Bernie had let us see a copy of the preliminary. I stressed the tentativeness of the findings until all of the tox reports were complete, and finished by saying, "Bernie has been our only police help over here. If I get too explicit they will know he gave it to us. They'll know we didn't call the coroner's office in Portland and get this much out of them. I'd hate to get him in trouble. I'd hate worse to get me in trouble with him." He grumbled some more, but finally agreed to give it another day or so.

At Sherry's insistence I called a cab. The phone rang twice, then there were some mechanical noises on the line and it rang in a different fashion. It was answered almost instantly by a feminine voice. I could hear motor noises in the slightly hollow sound of the cell phone. I gave her my number at the Gull, but that wasn't enough. She wanted my name and where I was going. I guess this was so she could schedule her runs or at least I hoped that was the only reason. I told her we were going to Long Beach, round trip. She said fifteen minutes.

It was over half an hour later when we saw her yellow top light crawl across the bottom of the window and she honked us into action. Sherry didn't waste any time. She said, "Take us up to the bank at Long Beach and wait. We'll be coming right back." She then began playing friendly. "You always drive at night?"

"Mostly," that was mostly a grunt.

"Don't you run into a bunch of weirdoes out at night?" Receiving only another grunt she continued, "I don't think I would have the nerve to pick these people up. People I didn't know, and take them to all kinds of lonely places."

This warmed her a bit. I personally didn't think she would have much to worry about. She wasn't very big, but the worn and dirty fatigues she was wearing were. Black hair framed a ferret face with protruding teeth. I'd guess the hair would entirely cover the face if she didn't occasionally apply a razor. The eyes were hidden by the bill of the cap. Her in the front seat and me in the back seemed perfectly normal to me. There would be no inclination to change it. She admitted to meeting some odd ones. Sherry asked if she drove on weekends with, "That would probably be the worst time of all."

"I work six nights. I like to work Friday and Saturday nights. That is when the big tippers are out. Haven't missed one in almost a year."

We had reached the light at Long Beach and Sherry waited for the woman to make the turn and then tossed in nonchalantly, "Then you must have worked the night the Finn was killed, did you haul him home from the tavern?"

The driver pulled into the bank parking lot and stopped. She turned in her seat and looked at Sherry, and asked, "Aren't you the lady lawyer? The one who is trying to get that crazy who killed him, off?"

"We are just trying to get at the truth. So, apparently you did take him home?" Receiving no answer she asked, "All we want to know, is what time did you take him home?"

"I don't have to answer your questions."

"Not right now, you don't. But you will have to answer when I subpoena you into court. You will have to answer the police questions if I tell them you know something about the killing and are refusing to tell us."

I threw in, "I noticed Bernie's car behind the cop shop as we came by. Why don't we pull around the corner and ask him if he doesn't want to ask you now?"

"All right. So, I did take him home that night. So what? I took him home lots of nights."

"So what shape was he in?"

"Same as always… Had to have help getting out to the cab."

"OK," Sherry said. "That wasn't so hard was it? What time was it and who helped him?"

"I don't know exactly without my log. It wasn't real dark yet so it must have been sometime shortly after five."

"And the helpers?"

"Just a couple of the regulars at the tavern. Probably someone he had been buying drinks for all afternoon. I think one of them was a guy named Riser. They probably rolled him on the way out to the cab."

"Thank you. Now you can take us back to where you picked us up." It was a silent ride. At the Gull I paid her and added a tip that Sherry raised her eyebrows at. As she alit from the cab, Sherry added, "Oh, about that log. Nothing better happen to it. If you don't have it when you get into court, you can go to jail for destroying evidence."

CHAPTER SEVENTEEN

We went back to our mental ping-pong. After I added the few bits we had picked up from the cab driver to the computer file, it always stopped at the same place. We didn't have enough to put it all together. I rearranged the file to create a timeline. It was interesting, but changed little. There was a window of almost three hours, between the time Suolo got home and Jimmy went there the last time, in which any number of people could have visited the isolated trailer without anyone noticing. At least anyone we were able to ask about it.

I finally threw in the towel with, "We are going round in circles. We need to be able to question these people so we can figure out who was where during those hours. We don't have enough authority to force them to talk to us."

"I can subpoena them…"

"That's after we weed them out. You can't drag half of Ocean Side into court. We need to get the cops into it. Let them chop a few weeds for us."

"They aren't really interested. Easley has Jimmy and he won't do anything to mess up the easy case he figures he already has against him."

"Maybe we should talk to Bernie, get him to ask some of the questions. He doesn't seem to be on Easley's side in this."

"I'm the defense attorney. I'm supposed to be able to ask the questions I want answers for."

"It's for sure, the answers are at the Safehaven. It's only a couple of blocks... We could maybe just walk over there and start asking questions. Didn't make us too popular the last time we went there, but we can try again if you'd like."

Sherry shuddered, and said, "That wasn't very nice." After a long silence she added, "Maybe you are right. Maybe Bernie would be a good idea. He doesn't seem too interested in helping the county prove their case."

We finally agreed to call him early the next day, and I offered to buy dinner at the Bar View. Sherry bought the idea of food, but only after a low remark about my selecting the Bar View, because I wanted to get my ego stroked. I suggested walking across, but Sherry said it would probably be raining when we wanted to come home, so we drove her car the block and a half.

The stars were out for a change, but as usual when it is clear, it is cold. There was a slight breeze from the north that didn't help except it blew the fish plant smells out over the river instead of over the town.

The restaurant was bright after the darkness. The back portion was closed off so the three occupied tables were just half of those available. All three of the window seats were taken. I didn't see anyone I recognized, but from their actions, the four people at the first table were aware of who we were. We continued on and took the back table of those open.

The waitress, one I had seen before, undoubtedly has a name, but I had never heard it. She dropped menus and filled our coffee cups. We were still discussing the options when the door opened again and Cleave ushered Desiree in. They stopped, blinking at the lights, and he pointed to the table next to us. She stopped, lady like, and waited for him to lead. She was wearing a dress and looked quite nice. He pulled out her chair, seated her facing us, and took the seat with his back our way without ever seeing us. She acknowledged us with a half smile and an equally short wave. Cleave saw it and turned to see who was behind him and caught me returning the gesture.

I expected some flack, but he just looked. No smile. No frown. Just a look. Sherry caught it also and turned his way. She was good. With a barely perceptible pause she said, "Hello Cleave. Desiree. Nice night for a change. What brings you two out?"

Cleave actually blushed. It was then I noticed: He was clean-shaven and clean dressed, as was Desiree.

She said, "It's our anniversary, of sorts. We have been together two years today."

Sherry drew a small laugh with, "Sort of like us, only he wouldn't remember." She continued to push the conversation. Using small talk to create the feeling we were all old friends. Desiree answered self-consciously, but only when cornered. Cleave did a lot of squirming, but almost no talking. I wasn't much better. I half expected her to invite them to join us at our table.

The waitress reappeared and we hadn't even opened the menus. Sherry asked for a few minutes and as soon as the woman left she asked, "You two probably eat here more than we do, what is good?"

Desiree said, "Most of the time we just have hamburgers, but when we want a good dinner, we have the chicken fried steak."

The information wasn't news. We usually ate the same thing. I knew that was what I was going to order when we arrived and I am sure Sherry would have done the same, but she was doing a masterful job of drawing them into the circle. She thanked Desiree and when the waitress returned, asked for a chicken fry in a loud enough voice to be heard at the next table. I half expected her to order four and have them all put on our tab.

While we ate, the people at the other three tables finished and departed. The group by the door who had noticed us when we came in stopped by the next table briefly. It was obvious we were part of the guarded conversation. As they were leaving they said they were heading for the tavern, thereby establishing why they knew us, and asked Desiree if she would be over. They received a definite maybe in answer.

Sherry never eats all of a meal, but she did that night. I'd swear she timed it to the opportune minute. She pushed her chair back and with a sigh, said, "Great food," loud enough to reach the others. Then she turned and said, "Thanks Desiree," receiving a full mouth nod and half wave in response.

We sat and sipped at our coffee. I have this automatic response. A full stomach and a little inactivity and my eyes get heavy. I began thinking of a soft seat and getting my shoes off, and figured Sherry would be on the same wavelength. She proved me wrong by turning to the other table at almost the exact moment they finished their food. She said, "You know we have been looking into this murder." Receiving wary nods, she added, "We saw a copy of the autopsy report today," which piqued a little interest. "The doctor said he thought Suolo was probably killed by something other than the maul. Meaning someone besides Jimmy."

Desiree asked, "What did he think it was?" Cleave just looked more uncomfortable and flashed her a look that said shut up.

Sherry ignored Cleave and answered, "Some sort of poison. He won't be sure until they do some more tests. It will be several more days before we will have the final report." She paused to let that sink in and then continued, "We are just trying to find out where people were last Friday night. To see who had the opportunity. Were you at the Safehaven?"

Neither moved for a moment and then Cleave said, "Younger wouldn't like it if we...."

Desiree cut him off with, "To hell with Younger. All he cares about is your money. He's your friend as long as you are spending." Turning to Sherry she said, "Yes, we were there."

"Who else was there? Who was tending bar?"

"Helen was until five when Melannie relieved her. I didn't really notice when she left the tavern. Younger came back from doing the banking about that time. He is usually around when Melannie works."

"Okay, Helen went home sometime about five o'clock. Did either of the other two leave the tavern any time before or about then?"

"I didn't pay that much attention. Younger spends most of his time in his office. I suppose he could slip out without being noticed. But out and back by the front door. Not likely. Everybody watches who comes in the front door. And I didn't say Helen left. She always stays for her free house drink, and then usually stays as long as her tips last and does a lot of socializing."

"She was probably there until about seven or maybe a little before." Turning to Cleave she asked, "Wouldn't you think about seven?"

He contributed a not very loud nod.

I remembered when we waited for her at the joint up the street. Probably while she took care of her free drinks. I decided to get into the action. I said, "We know from the cab company records that they sent Suolo home at about five-thirty. Did you notice who helped him to the cab?"

After a brief discussion between themselves, they came up with two names, Gordon Riser and Bert Roth, and added that both had been drinking with him all afternoon. I asked if either Younger or Melannie had gone out to the cab with them. Another conference and they said they were sure neither had done anything beyond calling the cab.

I didn't quite follow the reasoning when Sherry threw in, "How about Helen, did she help or was she involved?" She got the same answer.

I began making an exit, blaming the surplus of good food for making me sleepy. I didn't need to fake it too much. Sherry got in one final shot by asking, "Did you notice anyone talk to Younger or Melannie, and then leave for a while and come back?" She received nothing but puzzled head shakes.

I threw tip money on the table and pushed back, saying, "Hey this old man is pooped. Let's take him home to bed." I'm not sure Sherry was really ready to give it up, but she didn't argue. With a lot of "thank yous" and warm fuzzies we left them to their now cold food and walked up to pay our check. I asked the waitress what their fanciest and gooiest desert was. She said pie with ice cream was as fancy as it gets. I told her to add a pair to our check and deliver them to the other table. She took my money, but was still looking confused as we went out the door.

It was some sort of record. We had been in the restaurant about an hour and a half, and the weather was still clear and cold. About half way home a jacked up four by four with a light bar across the roof growled down the street toward the Safehaven. It was dark enough out that it is doubtful they noticed who we were.

I went to the computer to update our file. After staring at it for several minutes it dawned on me, all we had learned at the restaurant was what we didn't want to hear. We could prove that most of the major players, the people who we figured to hang it on, had alibis. I smelled hot and turned around. Sherry had turned on the heat, kicked off her shoes, and was lying on her stomach on the bed, elbows supporting her head, watching me. A most inviting picture.

I thought seriously of turning off the computer, but instead asked, "We didn't do that much good?" At her head shake I added, "Not much to add to the file. What did she say those guys' names were?"

"You mean you didn't have your tape going?"

"We just went there to eat… I didn't think I would need it." Actually it hadn't even entered my mind. "The only name I can remember is Bert."

"I keep telling you, you need to work on your memory so you don't need the tape recorder. The names were Gordon Riser and Bert Roth."

I punched them into the computer without comment, then picked up the local phone book. Neither was listed, even assuming the Bert was short for Albert. I said, "Pair of fine upstanding citizens. Neither is permanent enough to have a phone listed." Not that it would make any difference; addresses aren't listed in the book, beyond the town of residence.

Sherry said, "I'm bushed. Think I'll take a shower and sack out."

I gallantly offered to wash her back, but was turned down again. Getting to be a habit. I stared at the computer screen for the next few minutes, willing it to change to something meaningful, but nothing moved. The bath door opened and Sherry had on her usual sleeping attire. I vowed to get some new smaller Tee shirts. My extra larges just covered too much territory. Small would be much nicer.

By the time she reached the bed I had the computer off and was headed for the bathroom. On the way I flicked the thermostat down and killed most of the lights. No use making the people at the PUD too happy. I made a quick trip of it and crawled between the covers. I snuggled up and slipped a friendly hand around the warm body and cupped my favorite toy. Nothing is so firm and at the same time so soft and silky. Nor tastes so sweet. Sherry said, "I couldn't. I'm still stuffed. Why did you let me eat so much?"

I didn't figure she expected an answer. But I don't give up easily. I didn't relinquish any territory and after a few minutes tried a slow massage of the lovely I was holding. Without a word she turned firmly onto her stomach. I knew then the battle was lost.

Sherry was sleeping minutes later, but I wasn't as lucky. I lay and mulled over the few facts we had put together. Not much for five days. It must have been after eleven when I finally joined her.

The crash brought both of us up out of our sleep. My first thought was that it must be morning as the room was so light. The next one was fire because there were so many yells and all the flashing light coming from outside. The second crash I recognized. It was the old brick against the door routine, same as last time they visited me in the middle of the night. It was followed by another round of raucous yells.

My feet hit the floor, but I could get no farther. Sherry had a death grip around my middle and her face buried in my back. I turned and put an arm around her and said, "Easy honey, I don't think they got the guts to come in." I hoped she believed me. Hell, I really wasn't sure I believed me.

I finally quieted her enough to extricate myself and slipped over to the window. With two of us in residence, damn thing was steamed up more than the last time. When I wiped it off, I was sure those outside would know I was peering out. Maybe they were out of bricks.

Finally, screwing up my courage, I made a fast swipe with the end of the curtain and grabbed a quick look. I was sorry I had bothered. There were two jacked up trucks facing the window with headlights and roof lights blazing. Apparently, one had entered from each end of the circular drive and both were focused on my window. They were alternately goosing their motors and stomping their brakes, producing a lot of noise and smoke and making the trucks rock, but so far they weren't jumping them at the front of the building as they had done the other time. The light spilling off the side of the building showed shadowy figures in the back of both trucks. Assuming two or three in each cab, that meant eight or ten drunks, each trying to out bad ass the next.

CHAPTER EIGHTEEN

Guess Sherry decided the bed didn't offer a lot of protection because she joined me at the window. I pulled her back into the shadows, afraid someone would get the bright idea of lofting a brick through the glass. I asked, "You suppose this is what Bernie was talking about when he warned us these cretins could get ugly?"

"I don't think you're a damn bit funny. Maybe now is the time we should call him."

"He's home in bed. Time he could get here these jerks will have had their way with us and be long gone. You should have picked one of the local redneck hunters for a partner. They all got guns. I'd give anything for a shotgun about now." The motors continued to roar, with the drivers beginning to wind them up and pop the clutch, making the trucks bounce and jump forward as they had done the last time. It was getting critical as a couple more jumps would have them pushing on the wall and I had little faith in its ability to hold out against the bumpers.

I looked again as another set of lights came into the drive behind the first truck. I didn't say anything to Sherry as she was scared enough, but I thought, oh shit, reinforcements, this will set them off for sure.

Then the red and blue lights began to flash off the ceiling. It suddenly got quiet out front. I rose up and wiped the window clear just in time to see the second truck start to back out. Then there were headlights and more red and blue lights behind it.

Curiosity overcame her terror and Sherry joined me at the window. We were wallowing in the feeling of relief when I began to notice the cold. I said, "I guess we owe the local cops another thank you, but it would probably be more proper if we were rescued with some clothes on." Sherry looked at all of the legs she had hanging down from my Tee shirt and ran for the bathroom. She left me standing in the cold without even a Tee shirt.

I finally donned most of a normal quota of clothes and went out front to see what was happening. Officer John Robinson was supervising. The reserve officer who had been with Bernie at the Safehaven when they first rescued us was there again, and was reading the driver, standing with his hands cuffed behind him, his rights. He then informed him he was under arrest for driving under the influence. He then unceremoniously stuffed him into the cramped back seat of the patrol car. Sherry, now fully clothed and coiffed, joined me in the doorway.

I looked across to the other truck and recognized the bulky figure of Sergeant Malahovsky sitting quietly on the front fender of his car behind it. He waited patiently until the reserve came over and performed the same service for the driver of the second truck and deposited him in the deputy's car. The driver asked what was to become of his truck. Robinson answered, "It will be towed to the impound lot. Probably only cost you about a hundred dollars to pick it up after you bail out of jail tomorrow. That is if you have the proper papers. You know, license and proof of insurance." Knowing full well that chances were good he had none of the above.

The first driver began yelling they should let one of the other guys drive his truck home. Robinson turned to the men who had been herded into a group and said, "Be my guest, but be aware that any one of you gets behind the wheel of any vehicle tonight, you will get a driving under the influence citation and get to join those two in jail." There were six of them. They stood and muttered between themselves while the three officers wrote out citations for each of them for disturbing the peace. When they were allowed to go, they moved in a group toward the now closed tavern, but stopped on the sidewalk across the street to watch the finish of the show. I was sure our popularity with the tavern crowd had not grown too much tonight.

Robinson told them, "We will be around for a while. Any vehicle that moves in the vicinity of the Safehaven Tavern is going to be stopped. We have sufficient cause to believe the driver will have been drinking." A tow truck showed up shortly and he told the driver to take his pick as there was another on the way for the second rig.

As the tow truck turned up the street with its burden, the group on the sidewalk took advantage of the anonymity offered by the shadows to heckle and threaten the driver and his future on the peninsula. Malahovsky hit them with a spotlight and they suddenly lost all interest in the truck and began moving slowly down the street toward the tavern.

Robinson walked our way and I said, "Guess we owe you another one. Thanks again."

Never very talkative, he shrugged and grinned and said, "Definitely our pleasure, these are some of our favorite clients," as the deputy moved our way.

Sherry said, "You sure got here in a hurry." Then asked, "How did you know they were here?"

As the deputy joined us, Robinson answered, "We have been patrolling this area pretty regular lately, especially around closing time. When we saw this bunch loading up and making a lot of noise I called Steve for backup and we followed them over. Sorry it took so long, but we have been staying off the radios as much as possible because these guys all have scanners in their trucks, even though they are illegal. It took a while for him to get here and I didn't want to start without him because I didn't want any of them to get away." We stood silently and watched the second wrecker hook up the other truck.

Bob Nichols, owner of the Gull chose this time to join us. He was wearing a robe and slippers that I figured were mostly for effect as he'd had plenty of time to dress. He opened with, "This is getting to be a habit. This is the second time your friends have spoiled everybody's sleep. As I told you before, I run a quiet place where my tenants don't have to put up with this sort of thing."

I was sure the tenants were probably enjoying the little action in their usually boring lives, but I said, "They aren't friends of mine. I didn't invite them. We were sleeping just like the rest of you." I hoped he hadn't heard the bricks hitting the door. I didn't feel like paying for a new one.

Robinson tried to placate him by saying, "Come on Mister Nichols. It's not his fault. They are just a bunch of drunks from the tavern." After a remark about its never happening before I moved in, the fact that I have been living here for almost two years with no previous complaints was not mentioned, Nichols stalked away towards the office and his quarters. I was sure I would hear more about it later.

Sherry asked for the names of the drivers. Robinson said, "Oh, we know them pretty well. This one," indicating the first one who was in his car, "is Gordon Riser." The other name he mentioned was entirely unfamiliar.

I asked Sherry, "Why do I know that name?"

"That's one of the two who helped Suolo into the cab for his last ride." She didn't even zing me about my lack of memory, but her eyes told me she probably would have except for all the company.

I wondered, "Funny how the same names keep surfacing. It would be interesting to ask this guy if he were the anonymous caller who informed the police that Jimmy was the one who killed the Finn."

Robinson said, "I'm sure that could be one of the many questions we will be asking him tonight."

"We have a witness who heard mister anonymous bragging about making the call until Younger shut him up. She didn't put a name on him though. We didn't know at the time it would be important or we might have pushed it more."

Sherry asked me, "Who you suppose got these guys started tonight?"

"Not too many choices. We questioned the lady cab driver. You pushed her pretty good. She may have talked to some of the tavern crowd. And Desiree and Cleave... But I don't think we did anything to get them riled. Yeah and who was tending bar tonight?" To Robinson I said, "You might add that to your questions for these two."

Sherry said, "There were the people from that other table. They knew we were talking to those two. If they went back to the tavern and talked about it… Anything could have set Younger off as suspicious as he is."

Robinson listened to his shoulder momentarily and said, "I've got to go. Guess I will have to haul Riser around with me until I have time to take him north."

Malahovsky said, "Why don't you just dump him in my car with the other one. They can keep each other company until you get back. They will be so uncomfortable in that little back seat that they may give us the answer to a few questions on their own. Or I can haul them to South Bend and let them blow on the machine when I check out, if you don't get back before that." We watched them transfer Riser and the two cars finally turned off their flashing lights and headed up the street towards Long Beach.

Suddenly it was so quiet we could hear the surf breaking across the jetty a couple miles away. I became aware of the cold as the other tenants decided the show was over and their lights blinked off one by one. Sherry's teeth were chattering as she stripped off her clothes and dove between the covers. I said, "No Tee shirt, I'll have to invite them back more often," and followed her.

She was rolled up in a tight ball and pushed her back into me and I could feel her trembling. "I was terrified. Just hold me." After a few minutes she added, "Maybe I should get into corporate or real estate law." I lay and held her wrapped in my arms as she gradually quit shaking and dozed off. There was no use my pointing out to her that she did all of the above already. Problem was there were not enough clients clamoring at her door for her to specialize. Besides, I knew she liked what she was doing and would probably be her usual self with daylight.

When I awoke I knew it was late. No phone was my first thought. Then I tried to move and discovered that both arms, still entangled under Sherry, were asleep. They were like two logs, connected to my body by extreme pain only. I must have made a noise as Sherry reared up, ready to defend herself. That solved part of the problem. My arms were free, but then I became aware of a more pressing problem.

She sat and laughed at me as I fought my way to my feet with no help from the two useless arms dangling with no control and headed for the bathroom. I shouldered the door shut and found I still had a problem. Neither hand would perform the necessary services, so I sat and enjoyed the relief of one pain while I inflicted more by trying to massage some life back into my arms.

When I came out, Sherry disappeared into the bath with a snide remark about my getting old. I sat on the edge of the bed and worked on my arms and listened to the gurgling of the coffee pot she had turned on. She returned shortly, still without clothes, and made a detour past the thermostat. With a savage stab at the wheel on top she said, "Damn, I wish you would leave a little heat on."

I was sure she had turned it up to ninety degrees at least, but was too distracted by her anatomy to comment. It always affected me that way when I watched the movement of that body, the firm breasts leading the way. The soft curves of the waist and hips, the long legs. Instant lust. I lured her over by saying, "My arms won't work. They are still asleep from where you slept all night on them." I moved them slightly and winced mightily.

She looked at me in disbelief, but moved closer, warily, and reached for my arm. I closed the trap. With both arms wrapped around her, she called me a less than complimentary name and struggled momentarily, but not very long when I began kissing one of those beautiful pink nipples. By the time I switched sides, I wouldn't have needed any arms.

Then the damn phone rang. I cursed myself for not unplugging it, and tried to ignore its clamor. I thought for a minute I would get away with it, but at about the third ring, Sherry groaned and pushed backwards. I dropped my lips down to the area of her navel and was working my way south. For two more rings I was sure I was winning, but she pushed away and said, "It could be important. You better answer it."

"They'll call back…. It's probably just Charley." Finally, I gave up and grabbed the phone. It was Bernie.

"Morning Ankus. What kept you? You couldn't have been that sound asleep."

"Morning Bernie." The thick in my voice wasn't from sleep, but he took it as such.

"Hear you had another late party at you place last night. I saw Robinson's report. He mentioned your questions, but said he didn't get back here for an hour or so and Malahovsky had already taken them to South Bend."

"Damn… It's my opinion we are getting close to figuring this thing out. That's why they keep getting all excited and sending out the troops. Well maybe we can get some answers if we ask around."

"Jesus, you're a slow learner. Every time you rattle their cage they snap at your head. One of these times we won't be handy and they will take it off at your shoulders and I'll have another murder on my hands. Okay. Hang tough. Don't do anything. I hate that drive to South Bend, and it really isn't my case anymore, but I'll go up and talk to them. Probably won't do any good, but I'd hate to have to investigate your untimely departure. They probably got a lawyer by now though and won't be doing any talking."

"Thanks Bernie. We'll wait here and stay out of trouble 'til we hear from you." I turned to Sherry, expecting to finish what we had previously begun, and asked, "Let's see, where were we," and discovered she was completely dressed.

She asked, "What did he say?" At my attempt to play it down to distract her, she said, "Come on, I've never heard Bernie talk so much. He must have said something."

"He said we should have learned by now that these people mean us no good and that we should quit pushing them. We should just stay here and wait until we hear from him. He's going to run up to South Bend and question those two goons. I just figure he is right. And if we are staying here there is no reason we shouldn't enjoy our wait."

"It's after ten. I need to check in with my office." I sat and watched while she dialed her number and listened to her machine. She jotted down a couple of numbers and started to dial one of them. I interrupted to ask who it was and she answered, "It's my insurance friend." After a short conversation very little of it from her end, she hung up and said, "That's funny. Interesting kind of funny. He said he couldn't find any record of any insurance policy except for a couple of little ones that the banks hand out to account holders as freebies. That's only about ten thousand dollars. Not really enough to be a motive."

She dialed the second number and all I heard was, "Good morning this is Sherry Thompkins." A pause and, "OK. My office in an hour. See you there." To my questioning look after she hung up, she said, "The recently widowed. She wants to talk. Maybe we have finally got lucky."

CHAPTER NINETEEN

We emptied the pot before we left and still beat the hour by five minutes. But then I didn't take time to shave. I figured Melannie, in the circles she traveled, was used to a lot worse. She was late again.

She was thirty-five long minutes late when she cracked the door and with a worried look over her shoulder slid into the office. She was either very afraid, or a good actor. She looked at me for several seconds. I could see the wheels turn, as she decided whether or not I should be on the inside, then shrugged mentally and turned to Sherry and said, "I need you to be my lawyer."

"I am already representing Jimmy Beasley in the matter of your husband's death. It wouldn't be ethical for me to represent you also."

"It's not that. I'm afraid of Younger. He's already talking about spending my money and I'm sure he will hurt me if I don't give it to him."

Sherry said, "It's not your money until this murder is solved. It only took us a few hours to find out about Suolo's money. If he had put your name on the account, you might have been able to get enough for living expenses during the pendency, but I don't think that is the case. I'm sure the prosecutor took even less time to find it because he has all the powers of the police. He will have it tied up until you get a judge to let go of it, and that isn't going to happen until the matter of the death is settled."

"But I didn't have anything to do with his death. I was working that night. There are at least ten people who were there will vouch for me."

"As I said, I can't represent you as long as this murder charge is hanging over Jimmy. But I can give you some free advice. We got back the reports on your husband's insurance. He didn't have much. Maybe ten thousand, from what we could locate. The insurance company isn't going to pay even that until the cause of death and the who-done-it is settled. Younger is smart enough to know this. And he isn't going to hurt you as long as there is money in your future."

"He needs money now. He is about broke at the tavern. He borrowed money from some guys and he says they are threatening to break his legs if he doesn't pay up. If the liquor commission finds out he is mixed up with these people, he could loose his license."

I put in my oar with, "I thought he was doing pretty good at the tavern. Always seems to be a bunch of people from the cannery in there."

She looked at me for a long minute while she decided, then she said, "Drugs. Nose candy. He is dumb as hell. He sits back there and snorts coke all of the time. Probably at least a hundred dollars a day."

Sherry said, "I'd say you have two choices. You can go to Younger and make him understand there is no money until this is settled. He probably won't be happy, but he should be smart enough to know you can't change it. He might even gain some time from his creditors if he can convince them there will be a big payoff. The second choice is, you can go to a judge and get a restraining order to keep him away from you. That would mean you would have to get away from the tavern totally, and would put him on notice that he probably wasn't ever going to get any of the money."

"He would have me killed."

"Maybe, if you weren't involved, your best bet would be to tell us what you know and help us solve this whole thing." Melannie sank back in her chair. She sat immobile except for her eyes. They darted around the room and from Sherry to me as she considered her position. Sherry added, "I agree you will need someone to help you straighten out your inheritance. I will be happy to represent you as soon as we get the other thing out of the way."

After another protracted silence she finally asked, "What do you want to know?"

"We know most of it, but there are holes. We know that Suolo was drinking all day until you gave him the alcohol and knocked him out."

"How did you find? The alcohol was Younger's idea. I would never have thought of it." I thought, *Lady, you ain't about to admit you are too dumb to think of it unless you figure to gain by it.*

"And Younger went to the bank and ran into Jimmy at the service station where he told him Suolo was going to take back the truck. That's what got Jimmy started. He wouldn't have gone to the trailer at all otherwise."

"Yes he came back laughing about it. Thought it was a good joke. Until later when Riser came in and told him Jimmy killed Suolo. He was pissed. Ranting about our missing a chance to cash in. He started yelling that he had tried to tell me we should have bought some insurance on him and now it was too late."

I asked, "How did Riser find out?"

"He has been banging that woman who lives across the street from Suolo's trailer. Her husband goes up to Alaska fishing... Sometimes for six months at a time. He said he saw Jimmy go there. He was inside for a few minutes and then came tearing out like something was after him. Said the woman told him Jimmy was there twice earlier. Riser got curious and went over to check it out and found Suolo dead. He thought it was funny. He probably helped himself to anything that was loose in the trailer while he was there."

Sherry asked, "When did he suggest you buy this insurance on your husband?"

"Oh... I don't know...earlier.... Several times actually. One day when Helen was still working, she walked in on us and I'm sure she heard part of it."

Sherry gave me a knowing look and asked her, "Did Younger or anyone he talked to leave the tavern between about seven and ten that night?"

She thought a minute and answered, "Only Riser. He is the only one I remember. Maybe nine or nine-thirty he left. Then ten thirty or so he came back and told Younger that Suolo had been killed. He said offed, like some cheap movie. Younger sent him out to call 911 and tell them that Jimmy had killed Suolo. He was only gone a few minutes. Came back bragging about it until Younger shut him up."

By now I was glad I had my recorder. I was willing to bet she was telling the truth, whatever her motive, as what she was saying dovetailed into what we had already heard. I said as much, and then asked, "Do you remember what time Suolo left the tavern?"

"Let's see... Helen got off at five and I was working. Suolo started bugging me, so Younger started spiking his beer. Helen always has her after work drink and then any others that someone has offered to buy. She was still there. Probably between five and half past. I wasn't paying too much attention after Suolo got too drunk to bother me. We sent him home before long."

God, I wanted to unload on her. She obviously married the guy for his money, but he was bugging her when he tried to talk to her. I knew it would be the end of her cooperation through so I took a deep breath and asked, "Did anyone go home with him?"

"Riser had been sponging off him all afternoon. I think he helped get him into the cab, but he didn't go with him because he was there later. Probably rolled him for drinking money. I don't think anyone else left, but I'm not sure."

Sherry asked, "Is there anything else that you think we should know?"

"No. I worked all night. Even after... I think Younger was in his office all night. But then he has that little door that he can go out through the storeroom. He don't like it though as you have to walk along the side of the tavern on that little ledge over the water." She shivered at the thought and added, "He surely wouldn't do that at night."

Sherry surprised me by echoing my thoughts, saying, "I think that what you are telling us is the truth. Most of what you just told us we have heard from others or guessed. Yes, I'd be happy to represent you once this is out of the way. In the meantime, I don't think you need an attorney. Just tell Younger you checked and you can't touch the money until you are cleared. If he starts to get too nasty you can always go for a restraining order. If you intend to dump him later, you might start cooling things with him now though."

"I'm scared. He likes to see people get hurt. But I guess I don't have much choice. Thanks," and she slipped out the door much as she had entered. I thought, lady you were also drooling with him when you watched the action the night we were at the tavern.

Sherry sat for a minute and said, "I don't believe it."

"Don't believe what? I thought she was telling the truth and you told her the same thing."

"I mean the change. Just like that she goes from one side to the other. Two days ago we were the enemy and Younger was her protector."

"Greed or fear. Two good motivators. Take your pick."

After a moment's thought, I added, "It occurred to me when she was talking about the knee-cap breakers. Could it be possible they went up to see Suolo? Sort of help Younger raise some quick capital?"

"You have been watching too much television. There aren't any mobsters here on the peninsula." She didn't sound too sure of her statement. Just hopeful.

"Don't bet on it. The murder scene sounds like something a pro would arrange and we aren't that far from civilization. I've heard talk of others here on the peninsula with connections. There is a manager of a large motel on the peninsula who threatens people with his connections. He even has someone who calls him whenever the liquor commission is due to hit the town so he can straighten up his act."

"You've got to be kidding. You don't really believe it could be anything like that?"

"No I don't. Least not entirely. But you just agreed that we believe her, and she cleared both of our prime candidates. We are running out of suspects."

"She said Younger could have gone out."

"I wondered at her motives on that." We sat and mulled it over, but a half hour later we were no nearer to an idea. I finally said, "Everyone has some sort of alibi except that other bartender, what's her name, Helen, but I can't think of a possible motive for her unless she just wants Younger back, and I can't imagine how killing the Finn and making Melannie rich would accomplish that.

"Why don't we walk up to the bakery for a sandwich and the latest gossip? Maybe by the time we get out of there Bernie will be back. He is going to be pissed though. We got all of the answers he drove all the way to South Bend to get."

"You sick or something? You don't usually think of food."

The weather was still decent and there was almost no traffic as we walked up the street. The bakery was quiet. The locals, even in winter, usually work the early shift, leaving the place to the tourists by eleven or so. Midweek tourists, convinced there is nothing but rain on the peninsula in winter, stay away in droves. Despite the nice weather there was only two gray-haired couples in the place.

We decided on a bowl of clam chowder and split a sandwich. Out of habit, Sherry grabbed a window table while I paid. I enjoyed the food in spite of the fact that Sherry insisted the sandwich be stuffed with bean sprouts. Definitely not one of my favorites, and the window seats were a bust. There wasn't anyone on the street to watch.

When we walked out, Bernie's car was in front of the cop shop so we turned in. He wasn't in a good mood. He said, "That was a wasted trip. Somebody fronted them a lawyer after I left here and he told them to keep their mouths shut so I didn't get anything."

We told him about our visit with the new widow, pointing out that her story fit with those of two or three others we had talked with, and much to Sherry's disgust I let him listen to my tape. He grumbled a bit about lucky amateurs, but he did take some notes. About Helen being the bartender last night, he said, "That don't tell us anything. I can't really see anything she stands to gain from this whole thing. It just means the others didn't have to work so they had the whole evening to instigate."

He made no comment at the mention of outside gangsters, but I noticed his pen hand stop in mid air. Sherry asked, "There isn't any of that down here on the beach is there?"

"Not that we have ever been able to prove… But there are lots of drugs available on the streets and they have to come from someplace. We catch people with them from time to time, but they won't talk about where they got the stuff. But you better be damn careful nosing around if there is any truth in what she said. These locals can get nasty, but those guys play for keeps. Too many bucks involved. I keep telling you to let us handle it before you get hurt."

Sherry said, "I'm just trying to represent my client. You said they have taken it out of your hands and Easely sure isn't going to do anything to help. He is sure he has a winner in Jimmy."

The phone rang and Bernie turned to the desk and answered it. There was some small talk, which wasn't too enlightening when you only hear one end of the conversation and that's damn sparse. Then, "Yeah, doesn't surprise me. Who put it up? Thanks for letting me know." After signing off he turned back to us and said, "The County… Riser just made bail."

Sherry asked, "Who bailed them out?"

"Don't know where the money came from, but one of their drinking buddies showed up with a hand full of cash. It would have taken around fifteen hundred. Have to freeze a lot of fish for that."

Sherry said, "I'd nominate Younger, but Melannie said he was broke."

I said, "Chump change… He could probably rob the pool tables of that much."

"That gets us back to what I was trying to tell you guys before. Nothing happens in this town without someone seeing it. You are messing up Younger's getting his hands on the money. If he hears Melannie was up to see you, and you better believe he will, it's going to piss him off no end. Pardon my French Counselor, but it's time you got the message. Younger and his bunch are small town, but remember someone already got killed. If there is out of town muscle leaning on him, they are not going to take it too kindly if someone is messing with their chance of getting their money. Let the police handle it. I'd sure as hell hate to have to investigate two more deaths."

He stood up as he said it and I took it for a dismissal. I threw in, "We could have gone all day without hearing that again," as we moved out to the street.

CHAPTER TWENTY

It was a sobering idea. The actions of the local rednecks were worrisome, but they were all overt. Physical and dumb. Almost predictable. The thought of real professionals, people who might decide we were a threat to their business interests...someone who might cost them money. What steps they might take to eliminate that threat. That was something else. As my old daddy would say, "A horse with a different collar."

Back at my place, we added a few bits to the computer file and I printed out two copies. It didn't take long as there was less than two pages. We sat and stared at them silently. Nothing happened. This is where the light is supposed to flash.... Instinct is to point a finger at the all-revealing clue.... The only thing to move, the cursor on my computer screen, continued to blink maddeningly.

Sherry broke a long silence with, "It doesn't really say too much about drugs."

I wasn't sure if she was trying to convince herself there was no reason why we should worry about mob connections or if she was making a point. I said, "We have a list of what we know. It doesn't tell us much of anything. Let's make a list of what we don't know." At her questioning look, I posed, "Number one, we don't know if there were drugs involved. We suspect there must be and Melannie said Younger was hooked, but we don't have any definite proof."

She added, "If we don't know there were drugs, we don't know there was any mob involvement."

I thought that one answered my question. She was trying to convince herself there was no gang to worry about. But I wasn't dumb enough to say it. I offered, "We don't know where that other bartender, Helen, was, after about seven." We beat this about and came to the conclusion that it didn't make much difference, as she just didn't fit as a suspect anyhow. Not only did she not have an apparent motive, but she was nothing more than a bit player. No power that would get people to do malicious things to others for her.

She said, "OK, so how about Younger? Melannie said he could have slipped out of his office."

"I'm not sure I trust her motives, but I'll put it down. We don't know where he was for sure." Then, "There is also his flunky, Riser. We don't know exactly what time he went out roaming around either, but we do know he was at the trailer. Supposedly after the fact. But we don't know that for sure."

We were startled by a loud knocking at the door. A peek out the window revealed my landlord, trying to look very officious. I opened the door and without preamble, he said, "You are going to have to find someplace else to live. This is the second time you have caused a disturbance in the middle of the night and woke up all my tenants."

"I hope you don't think those people were any friends of mine. I certainly didn't invite them."

"All I know is that it doesn't happen with any of my other tenants. I want you to move."

Sherry pushed into the doorway and said, "Mr. Nichols isn't it?" Without waiting for a response she added, "I'm an attorney and you obviously are not conversant with the landlord tenant regulations. You are required to put this all in writing and have it served by a disinterested party. You must set forth the reasons and give a reasonable time for the tenant to move out. If the tenant doesn't do so you have to go before a judge to prove your charges and then get an eviction order which is served by the sheriff." Nichols had backed up at this unexpected attack. She followed with, "If you care to pursue this further, we will see you in court. I think any judge will agree that Mr. Hill here is the victim, not the transgressor. After all, they were all arrested and hauled off to jail. Good day Mr. Nichols." She turned and pushed me back into the room and shut the door on the red faced man who was standing in the thickening darkness, and the rain that I hadn't even noticed had begun anew.

"Hey lady… You turn me on when you use that lawyer talk. Why don't we hop into that bed and discus all of this in a more friendly atmosphere."

"You're always turned on and you have used that old one too many times. I'm hungry. Why don't we drive across the river and have a nice dinner where nobody knows us? A couple drinks and some soft music and you may convince me." I put up a halfhearted argument that I knew from the beginning I would lose. It was obvious we were done with the list. I did a quick shave and put on a clean shirt. We were about to go out the door when the phone rang.

Charley opened with, "Damn I don't believe it…! On the first ring." Leaving no room for answer, he asked, "I haven't heard from you, what's going on over there?" I told him about our visitors of the previous night and confessed that we really didn't have anything new so I probably wouldn't have anything for him for tomorrow. "Shit, the wire services seem to have given up also. I was sort of figuring on you to fill that big hole in the middle of the front page."

"You know Easley, if anything happens, he won't pass up a chance for the publicity. He'll give it to the wire people though, better mileage. And the TV if he can interest them." I didn't take the obvious bait. I didn't respond to his offer of the front page. He groused, but finally hung up. By this time I was beginning to be hungry myself. I started to shut off the computer and something grabbed me. I hadn't backed up my computer files since before I went to the restaurant several days ago. I told Sherry to wait and sat down and ran a quick copy of all of the files on the murder, the only thing of any importance I had added lately, and pushed the floppy between the pages of a book, in a pile of books on the table.

We followed Sherry's prescription. The setting was great; the restaurant was on piles and hung out over the river. Sort of reminiscent of the Safehaven, except without the grunge. Not fancy. I think the latest is, but chic funky. The food was so-so, the drinks were slightly more than a couple, and the music got nicer as the dancing continued and it got more friendly.

A couple of hours later when we made our slightly tipsy way to her car, she even made a lewd suggestion. I was willing, but after I wedged myself into the dinky little car I decided it wasn't practical. She whipped out of the parking lot and headed for the bridge. I hoped there were no cops around. I didn't want to join the local tavern crowd in the drunk tank. I was sure they wouldn't let us go coed.

She topped the bridge over the Columbia River and hit the down side. I could see no sign of another car in the over three miles of straightway ahead. The wipers, never very good on the sports car, were doing a lousy job on the rain streaked windshield, but the bright dial of the speedometer was only too visible. I watched fascinated as the needle swung smoothly around the large dial. When it passed the hundred mark, I tore my eyes away and concentrated on the blurry road ahead. I wondered briefly, how many G's we would be pulling when we leveled off at the bottom of the hill. Only briefly, because it was only seconds until we were there.

As we approached the rise at the Washington side, she snapped her foot off gas and we listened to the burble and pop as she shifted down and the car slowed on compression. I fully expected her to bust the stop sign at the bridge end, but there was a car coming from the right. She braked sharply and we sat and watched as her headlights lit up the insignia on the side of the Washington State Patrol car that was heading toward Ocean Side. I asked, "Who said there is never a cop around when you needed him?" and settled back for a more leisurely ride home.

Back at the Gull, it was a rerun of several other nights. All the lights were on and the door was slightly ajar. We sat in the car and watched the thin line of light. Nobody said anything for several minutes. I finally said, with more assurance than I felt, "Wait here, I'll check it out."

Sherry said, "Maybe we should drive to a phone and call the police."

Truth is I was in agreement, but my ego wouldn't let me do it. I quietly pushed the car door open and swung my feet out. Then I realized the damn courtesy light was on. I swear it lit up half of the parking lot. Nothing moved, so I slid the rest of me out and closed the door quietly. I stood and listened, but all I could hear was the TV in the next unit. I moved quietly over and peered in through the window. I could see nobody and nothing out of place, but I could only see about a third of the room.

I moved over and tried the door crack. I could see even less, but a different area, so I very carefully tried to ease it open further. How come I never noticed before? It squealed like the proverbial stuck pig, loud enough to alert anyone inside. I retreated to the car and stood and watched for what seemed an hour, but I'm sure was only several minutes. Nothing moved. I returned to the door, stood alongside it, and reached around the corner and pushed it wide open. There were no shots or other loud explosions. When nothing happened despite the squeal, I ventured in slowly. No guns went off and everything appeared to be in its usual place.

After a quick look, I motioned Sherry to join me. She took a worried look around and said, "Maybe you just didn't pull it all the way shut. There doesn't seem to be anything missing or broken."

I wanted to agree with her. The door doesn't always catch on the first try, but I was sure I didn't leave all the lights on. The earlier mood had evaporated, but I figured if I let it drop she would relax and I would work at regaining it. I turned off the bright lights and she sat on the edge of the bed and asked for a drink.

I went to the sink and fixed the drinks that neither of us needed and I was sure would never be finished. I started back toward her with a drink in each hand, when I damn near dropped them both. That someone had been in the room was confirmed. I hadn't noticed it with all of the lights on, but the red light on my printer was blinking malevolently. Someone had been in who knew enough about computers to have printed something, and I had little doubt as to what it was. But they had forgotten to turn off the printer.

Sherry caught my look and was immediately on her feet. She asked, "What is it? What happened?"

I tried to come up with a plausible lie, but could think of nothing. I finally answered, "Somebody has been into my computer. They left the printer on. I'm sure I turned it off before we left. Come to think of it, I didn't even use it. I wonder what they printed." With my clunky old word processor, the easiest method is to create a new directory with each new story I work, with everything pertinent as files in it. I had little doubt about where to look. I started through the files on the murder and found they no longer existed.

Some time ago I had accidentally erased half a novel I was working on. As a consequence I had installed a program that would retrieve deleted files. I had the copies I made before we went across the river, but I guess I was just mad and wanted to prove something. I thought, *You are not so smart. I'll just pop them back up.* I moved into the program and asked it to list any recently deleted programs. One by one I restored them. I then moved back into the word processor and popped up the file on what we did or didn't know.

It asked, "DO YOU THINK I'M STUPID?", all in caps. I'm not sure how, but some way, he had defeated my special program. One by one, I went through the other files. Nothing, until I hit the last one.

It said, again in caps, "YOU HAVE BEEN WARNED SEVERAL TIMES ABOUT DIGGING AROUND IN THINGS THAT ARE NONE OF YOUR BUSINESS. CONSIDER THIS A FINAL WARNING, FROM A FRIEND WHO IS TRYING TO SAVE YOU FROM SOME SERIOUS HURT. GO FIND SOME NICE SAFE STORIES TO WRITE ABOUT OR SOMEBODY IS APT TO BE WRITING YOUR OBITUARY."

At her gasp, I became aware of Sherry reading over my shoulder. She said, "If they wanted to scare me, they have certainly accomplished their purpose. Maybe we should pack up and go to my place or better still a motel for the night."

"I don't think they will be bothering us tonight. They will wait and see if we follow their directions. Besides, if they were going to do something to us, they would probably be watching right now and see where we went."

"Thanks. That makes me feel a lot better. I'm sure now I don't want to stay here. You really think someone is out there watching us?"

I mentally kicked myself for my choice of words as I went about locking up and turning off. What was it they used to say? Loose lips sink ships. I knew, as I jammed a chair under the doorknob and set a kettle on it, that my ship wasn't going to come in that night. Unfortunately, it turned out that I was only too right.

CHAPTER TWENTY-ONE

It was a long night. It was hours before Sherry quit fighting devils and quieted down so we both got some sleep. For the second morning in a row the phone didn't ring, so it was almost ten when I finally woke up. I slipped quietly out of bed, turned on the coffee, and headed for the bathroom. When I came out, Sherry was sitting cross-legged on the bed, holding the phone with her shoulder while she punched in numbers.

"Nothing. Just a couple of calls that didn't leave any message. How did we sleep so late, it's ten o'clock? I should have been in the office an hour ago," she said, as I watched the long legs disappear into the bathroom.

Minutes later, Sherry came out, fully dressed and ready to go. She was not too happy when she found me still in my nightclothes, or in my case, because of my preference for sleeping in the buff, lack of same. I pointed to the cup of coffee I had poured for her and suggested we should decide first what to do about our visitors of last night.

Her answer, "There isn't anything to decide. We go see Bernie," was delivered in a tone that left no room for debate. I decided last night's shave would last a while longer and dressed while I finished my coffee. I thought of calling to see if he was in his office, but didn't. It was ten-thirty when we loaded into the Z and headed up the highway. We were just leaving town when Sherry asked, "Where did he come from?"

It took a second to figure, she was eying something in her rearview mirror. I turned and looked out the back window. The biggest and blackest and meanest looking four-wheeler I could ever remember seeing was following a respectful hundred feet behind us. He looked like an escapee from a monster truck show. Like he could drive over the little sports car and maybe just get it's top dirty. Coincidence? I didn't think so, but he made no threatening moves.

The tenth avenue light caught us and he moved up close behind. All I could see out the rear window was the front differential and the bottom edge of the front bumper. With a bumper sticker stating, 'This vehicle insured by Smith and Wesson.' The license plate was local.

There was a space open in front of the cop shop and Sherry slid into it. The black truck went on by as if he weren't interested. The door was locked. I said, "We could walk up to the bakery and have one of those big cinnamon rolls. Maybe Bernie will be back by then."

Sherry repeated her earlier, "I should be in my office. Somebody is apt to be looking for me." But it was without much conviction, so we started up the street.

With a click of locks, the door opened. Bernie poked his head out and, "Counselor. Ankus. I was just going out. Something I can do for you?"

Hopefully, I said, "Yes, but I'll buy you a roll if we can do it over coffee."

He stepped back inside and held the door open, saying, "Like I told you before, I'm trying to lose this," as he patted his stomach. He moved back into the office and asked, "Now what can I do for you?" He listened to our account of last night and said, "Interesting. I don't imagine any of the people who hang out at the Safehaven know squat about computers. Sounds like maybe some sort of pro. Maybe out-of-towners. I read the reports from last night and nobody mentioned anything unusual, but a lot of tourists come and go so a strange car wouldn't be noticed unless they did something dumb."

Sherry asked, "Out of town? You mean you think drugs...? The mob?"

"We have known there are drugs available at that place for years, but we have never been able get inside. Everybody in a small town knows everybody else and any stranger is suspect. You guys have seen that well demonstrated."

I threw in, "Melannie said Younger was hooked on coke, but didn't say anything about where he was getting it. Maybe she is his supplier."

"Coke's not supposed to be addictive," he said with a wry grin. "Besides, Melannie has only been around a little over a year and we think it predates that." He was interrupted by an electronic beep that sounded loud in the small room. The fax machine began slowly spewing out curly sheets of paper. Conversation stopped as we all sat and watched it as if it were some new and unknown process.

Bernie stretched across and grabbed the first sheet when the machine released it. He glanced at it, threw it on the desk, and stood and hovered over the machine. I picked up the page he had dropped and showed it to Sherry. It was the cover sheet for the pages now arriving, and indicated the sender was the coroner's office from Portland.

Bernie snatched the next page off the machine and dropped it after a quick look. The next one, he ran one finger rapidly down the page as he read, and then he threw it on the desk. "That is just the same as we got before." The fourth page fell. He glanced at it and added a disgusted, "Damn... Didn't they ever hear of paper conservation?" He threw it atop the first three.

Toward the bottom of the fourth page, a paragraph had been added: *Partial results of the toxicology screen are now available. Besides the aforementioned high ethyl alcohol content of the subject's blood, methanol was also discovered. The fact that it was in its original form, IE, had not metabolized into formaldehyde, would indicate that it was probably administered by injection rather than oral ingestion. This would also explain some of the eye damage that we previously attributed to chronic alcoholism.*

Then he began to editorialize: *Curious choice. Could be either an amateur who thought it would not be detected as different than the ethyl already in the system or a pro who didn't care. In either case it had to have been administered very shortly before the death. Methanol will usually bring on a coma in fifteen minutes to a half hour. Death will follow shortly thereafter if medical help is not immediately available. These times could be shortened considerably by the excess ethyl alcohol already in this subject's system.*

By this time, Bernie had pulled a heavy book from his shelf and was thumbing through its well worn pages. He read, "Methanol, related to Ethyl Alcohol. Rubbing alcohol. Also found in antifreeze, paint remover, perfumes. A solvent for varnish or shellac. There is a list here as long as your arm. Anybody could have it under their sink. Toxicity 5…. That puts it right up there with arsenic."

He continued to read, "Can be swallowed, breathed as a vapor, or absorbed through the skin. I never realized before. That's some nasty shit." He went on to read two paragraphs of graphic descriptions of how the death would come about. None of it was pretty.

I said, "Poor old Finn. Never had a chance. He was already knocked out by the booze they fed him before they gave him the needle."

Sherry added, "That just about guarantees Jimmy Beasley didn't kill him. I should be able to take this to Judge Harriman and get him released."

Bernie asked, "Are you sure that's a good idea Counselor? There are a bunch of nuts running around out there and one of them still might think that if they eliminated him the whole thing would go away. I think he is probably better off where he is until we can name someone to take his place."

"I'll have to think about that. This makes it look more like someone might want to get to him. In the meantime can you make sure they keep him separated from the others up there?"

"Maybe I should put you two in with him. Keep you separated from the same people. I've asked the guys to spend as much time as they can in the Ocean Side area, but we have a lot of other places where we are needed. It is obvious these guys can get to you any time they want. I hate to keep saying it. No, damn it, I hate that you don't listen when I say it. You are going to keep nosing around and someone is going to get hurt."

"But I have to keep digging. I owe it to my client to prove what happened so I can prove he isn't responsible. You say it isn't your case anymore and the county isn't apt to waste too much time on it. Easley has his mind made up. Figures he has an easy conviction."

"You said that before. Maybe he has. But don't fool yourself, some of the deputies don't entirely agree with him. They are also spending a lot of extra time down in this area."

We thanked him for his concern and his help as we moved out of the office. I thought about the big truck we saw on the way up, but didn't mention it to him. Out on the sidewalk I took her arm and steered her towards the bakery and breakfast, but she resisted with the argument that she needed to be in her office. I knew her heart wasn't in it and it was about a half hour later before we were back in the car.

She looped around the block and zipped out into traffic, heading south, in front of a startled motorist who I'm sure made a few less than complimentary comments. I thought we were heading for her office, only a couple of blocks down, but she didn't stop. At my question, she said she was taking me back to my place, as she didn't think I would want to sit around her office all day while she worked.

We had gone perhaps a half-mile when she said, "Where the hell did he come from?"

When I realized she was looking into the rearview mirror again, I turned and looked out the back window. The same black truck was in the process of passing a car, in a no passing zone, to become the third rig behind us. I felt a cold chill and said, "Same one." Feeling dumb about my obvious comment, I added, "This is too many coincidences for one day."

Sherry said, "I didn't see him until he passed a couple of other cars back there. Must be trying to catch up with us." She started picking up the speed. When we hit the forty-five mile per hour sign at the edge of town, we were already doing over fifty-five. The truck almost ran a northbound car off the road, as he passed the two in between us. Sherry kept her foot on it and continued to accelerate as we bore down on

Black Lake. The little car didn't stand a chance against the monster engine of the truck and he had a running start on us so he continued to gain. The road makes a ninety to the right at the lake and it was coming up fast. So was the truck.

Sherry downshifted and slowed on compression, hit the brakes briefly, then turned left abruptly as the truck reached about two car lengths behind us. She then accelerated so the car went into a slide and whipped off to the left. The tires squalled and we slid sidewise momentarily. The tires finally gripped and we shot off into the narrow entrance of Sandridge Road.

I released my breath and looked out the back. I was just in time to watch the truck as he tried to follow. The plan was obvious. Just a small nudge in the corner, at our speed, would have sent us rolling. With no railing on the road, we would end up in the lake. It's a small lake, but big enough. I'd hate to quote odds on our survival.

Expecting a right turn banked for forty-five, the driver was surprised when we turned left into a twenty-five mile an hour corner, actually banked the wrong way. He tried to follow. Half way into the turn he panicked and hit his brakes, lost traction, and began to slide sidewise. He tried to correct. The wheels finally dug in and the top-heavy, jacked up truck, as if in slow motion, started to roll. The second roll was faster and brought him to the lake bank where he went airborne for about thirty feet and went end over end. He landed, upside down and nose first, in the water with a huge splash. All that was left was a cloud of dust hanging over the road and a widening circle of waves coursing across the water, and as the truck settled, around one rear wheel that was sticking up. It had looked like slow motion, but had only taken seconds until he was gone.

Sherry had been watching in her mirror. She calmly pulled the car to the edge of the road, turned off the key, and sagged in her seat. She sat staring straight ahead. With my usual lack of finesse, I said, "Jeeze lady…. You probably saved our lives. We could have been the ones in the lake. Where did you ever learn to drive like that?"

It was my usual hoof in mouth response. She didn't move except for sinking lower in her seat if that were possible. Then she began to shake and the tears started welling up in her eyes and spilled slowly down her cheeks.

I reached across and pulled her as far as I could into my arms. She didn't resist, nor did she help. Not for the first time, I cursed the bucket seats and the center console that so effectively divides the car.

After an interval that seemed endless, she reached across and put her arm around me and her head on my chest. She started to sob and her body twitched with intermittent shivers. I realized this had been coming on for days. She had appeared calm, but really was so terrified that she was running on nerve alone. It was quiet where we were so I just sat and held her. The first of several sirens arrived at the lake behind us, but I don't think she even noticed.

CHAPTER TWENTY-TWO

Sitting there holding Sherry, I must confess, was not where I wanted to be. I couldn't actually see what was going on behind us in either rearview mirror, but there were reflections of red and blue flashing lights in every polished surface of the car. Unfortunately, my camera was back at my place, but a saleable story was happening right behind me and I wanted in. I realize that doesn't make me mister nice guy. Just an old reporter.

Sherry was quieting and my arm was about to fall off when I heard crunching in the gravel behind us. Sherry tensed up and when the knuckles rapped on the window she gave a little scream and almost jumped in my lap. I turned and could only see the stomach, but recognized Bernie's bulky figure. I pushed the door open and he asked, "Are you guys all right?"

"Sherry is a bit shook up, but otherwise we weren't touched."

"What the hell happened? The people in the car that was behind you said it looked like they were trying to run you down with that truck."

"Sort of looked like that from in here also. What's going on back there? What do the guys in the truck have to say about it?"

"One of them isn't saying anything. He is still down there. Pinned under the truck is my guess. They took the other one to the hospital. I wouldn't give him very good odds. We still aren't sure which was the driver. I assume it was the guy in the hospital as the registration is in his name."

After Sherry assured me she would be OK, I slid out and walked back toward the lake with Bernie. On the way I told him about our seeing the big truck on the way up. This drew a disapproving frown, but he didn't say anything. I outlined the trip back and told him that if Sherry had continued on down the highway, turning right instead of left, we would probably be the ones being fished out of the lake.

By this time we were standing on the bank watching as the volunteer firemen floundered around the truck in the cold water. Somewhere in all of this, clouds had moved in from the ocean and a fine, but no less wet, cold drizzle had begun. One of the truck tires was still just poking out of the water. Bubbles and patches of oil were still popping to the surface. Living up to its name, the lake's water was so black nothing else was visible. Several swans who winter over in the lake were cruising in circles on the other side of the lake and warily eying the commotion in their usually quiet waters.

We had to move aside as a wrecker backed up to the edge of the water. We watched as a fireman passed the cable and its hook out to a fireman in the water who in turn gave it to a man in a small boat. Another fireman managed to get it hooked to something below the surface of the water and the winch began to grind slowly.

The water started to swirl and then gradually the rig appeared. Bernie cupped his hands and yelled, "Hey Jeff." The man in the boat looked up and answered. Bernie said, "How about putting a marker down. We are going to have to get divers down there as soon as possible. I called the rescue volunteers when I first got down here and they should be here shortly. Be a lot easier for them to find if the location is marked."

The truck was coming up back end first. The bumper sticker on this end said, "Go ahead and honk, I'm reloading."

I felt a small hand slip into mine and became aware of Sherry standing beside me. She didn't say a word. Just stood and stared as the truck came out of the black water. A shudder went through her when the truck finally came high enough to see that it had lost its right side door. One of the men yelled up to inform Bernie there was nobody inside.

I asked, "You have any names yet?" Bernie's look said I shouldn't be asking, so I explained, "Just wondering where they fit into the puzzle… If they were some of people we know from the things at the Gull." Really I was thinking, *if I would hurry, I could still make Charley's deadline. Make him happy and me a couple of bucks.*

"The one we think was driving is your friend Riser. Least it's his truck." I asked Sherry why that name was familiar. She reminded me he was one of those arrested at the Blue Gull as well as the one who found the Finn's body. Obviously, someone had come forward with his bail money and money to get his truck out of impound. I was sure it wasn't the Alaska fisherman's wife.

After a huddle with the other two cops on the scene, Bernie said, "I'm going up to the hospital. See if I can get anything out of Riser. Maybe shook up enough to say who put him up to this." I suggested maybe we should go along with him, but he said, "I don't think that will be necessary, I still know how to question a perp." From his expression I knew I would lose the argument, so I didn't push.

The drizzle was beginning to penetrate my bones, but we stood and stared with the growing crowd. Not very much happening on the peninsula during the winter so any diversion is appreciated by the locals. I sometimes suspect mental telepathy, the way the word always gets around. Or maybe it's the plethora of scanners that does the job. Finally, Sherry said, "I'm cold and getting damned wet. They don't need us here."

We were almost to the car when I spotted a familiar figure. Desiree, my almost friend from the Safehaven. She was walking down between the cars stacked up on the highway where the drivers abandoned them to join the gawkers at the lake. The peninsula doesn't even have traffic jams like this during the height of the tourist season. I pointed her out to Sherry and we waited for her to walk up. After the niceties she asked, "What happened anyway?"

Her boyfriend Cleave hove up behind her as I answered, "Couple of guys decided to wash their truck the hard way." The truck chose this time to slide over the lake bank. It was on its left side, with the top toward us and didn't look anything like it had a few minutes earlier.

She asked, "They know who?"

"They think a guy named Riser was driving, his truck anyway. He went to the hospital. Other one isn't going anywhere, he's still down there."

"Karl Hall. That's who was with him. At least he was with him earlier today."

"How do you know that?"

"We saw them sitting in the parking lot down the street from The Blue Gull. Some time around nine this morning." She responded to an elbow and a dirty look from Cleave by adding, "What difference does it make now? He is dead."

"But there are enough who aren't. Somebody will carry the word back to the tavern. And who it was they saw talking to these people."

"They can go to hell. I don't want any part of this mess and I will talk to whoever I want."

"Somebody goes back and tells them we were talking to these two and we could end up in the river," and Cleave started to walk around us toward the lake.

The lawyer finally kicked in. Sherry moved in front of the big blonde and said, "I'm sure you know more about this. We are sure they were trying to kill us. We need to know who is behind it. Who put them up to it."

"Cleave is right. We could be in trouble...."

"You could be in more trouble if you withhold evidence." The woman started to push on by and Sherry asked, "Would you rather talk to the police?" At the lack of reaction she added, "I could take you in front of a judge and he would make you tell us."

Sherry was not her usual cool self. Her nerves were obviously getting to her. Her voice kept rising and was becoming strident. I gripped her arm and said, "Please, Desiree, we need your help. We think there have been about three attempts on our life. All we need is a few answers from someone who knows what goes on at the Safehaven." She hesitated, flushed, and began to move on. I asked, "Isn't there someplace we could meet you?" And watched her back as she walked away.

After we reached the car, I looked back. There were two men with wet suits walking over the lake bank, flippers in hand. The divers had arrived to perform their grisly task. Sherry started the car, and at my suggestion of nosing around the hospital to see what we could find out, she said, "It's only a block or so, we should have walked. We will never get through that crowd now." But she swung the little car around and drove slowly down the shoulder toward the mess.

The two cops had begun trying to sort out the snarl, but most of the drivers were out of their cars and most of the rest were in no hurry to leave. One of them saw us coming. I'm not sure if he knew us as friends of Bernie, or was just happy to get one car out the way, but he waved us through. The hospital was only a short two blocks away, but there was no way we could make a left turn. My thought of taking the back way to it was shot when we passed the street where we would need to come back. The line of cars snaking up over the hill to mingle with the jam made it obvious there were a lot of locals who came up with the same idea. The road ahead was clear of cars and apparently our only option. Luckily, the Gull was three blocks in the right direction.

First thing I did was call Charley and offer him the story. I didn't give him our involvement, but told him we had names of the occupants and there were some rumors that they were attempting to run someone off the road. "I don't have any art." At his grousing, "I was not in my own car. But I can send you a couple thousand words in an hour or so, and I'm sure it has a tie in to the murder thing."

"You know I'm right on deadline now." But I knew he would hold a hole for it.

I hung up the phone and turned to a blast from Sherry. "Is that all you ever think about? We were just almost killed and you just can't wait to see it in the paper."

She started to cry. I took her in my arms and said, "Sorry babe, but that's what I do. By three this afternoon some stringer will have it out on the wire service. By five, every TV station around will be down here because the stringer will hint that it has something to connect it to the Finn's murder. By six this evening my story will only be good for wrapping fish. What's the legal term? Time is of the essence. Sort of like you have to be in front of the judge on his schedule, not yours."

She quieted and I could feel her slowly relax. I was beginning to wonder if she were going to sleep when she pushed away and said, "All right, go write your damn story."

I held on for a few minutes more just to prove I thought of other things besides the story. Actually, I was mulling over the lead for my piece. 'A local four by four went airborne'... 'After flipping three times'... 'One man died and another'.... I finally released her and said, "Why don't you call the hospital and try to get hold of Bernie? Tell him the name of the second guy and also tell him about the truck watching the Gull before they followed us this morning." As I turned on the computer I noticed the time. It was still barely afternoon.

When the processor came up on the computer I started to tack out a story for Charley. I could hear Sherry arguing with the hospital switchboard as she tried to get through to Bernie. I tried to shut it out and concentrate on my story. I used to be able to ignore the restrained chaos of the city room at deadline, but that was a few years ago. She apparently won the argument because she stopped talking and sat waiting. I found I still had trouble as I was sitting and waiting for her to talk to someone also.

Some people can do two things at once. Not me. I have trouble enough with all of my brain. Half a brain won't cut it. I finally got focused and the words began to flow onto the screen. Sherry must have reached Bernie because she started talking again in a low voice. I realized I was straining to hear her instead of focusing on the task at hand. She cradled the phone momentarily, and then announced she was checking her machine and picked it up again.

Able to ignore this, I was well into the second of what I planned to be four pages when the phone rang. Sherry picked it up, listened a minute, and passed it to me mouthing, "Charley."

He opened with, "Where the hell is this big story you were going to send me?"

"It's only been a half hour. The phone keeps interrupting, and I can't get anything done."

He mumbled something about smart-assed reporters, and you used that on me before, and then said, "It's going to be funny looking paper if I don't get it pretty soon." I'm sure he meant to jab me in the wallet when he added, "A third of the front page will be blank." With a click he was gone.

Not taking chances of any more phone call interruptions, I dropped the receiver on the floor. Sherry had curled up in a ball on the bed so I pulled the blanket across her and went back to work.

The damn phone was still trying to get my attention. It kept protesting in a loud metallic voice and demanding I dial a number or hang up. I unplugged it.

Twenty minutes later I ran the spell checker over the piece, re-hooked the phone, and sent it happily across the river.

I sat back, seriously contemplating joining Sherry. The phone rang and Sherry reared up and looked wildly around. Thinking it was Charley with a problem with my story, I picked it up, and it asked in a small voice, "Mister Hill?" At my admission that I was he, the voice said, "This is Desiree Bennett. Mister Hill, what do you want from me?"

CHAPTER TWENTY-THREE

It was not a call I expected and my actions reflected it. I stammered, "Uh, hello. You caught me by surprise." To let Sherry know who it was I added, "Yeah Desiree, we had a couple questions we'd like answers to, but I didn't think you would talk to us." Sherry came scrambling across the room, twisted the phone out from my ear, and she pressed her face in beside mine. Afraid she would speak up and spook the woman, I covered the mouthpiece and shushed her, and received a look that asked if I thought she was dumb or something.

Desiree said, "Cleave is really paranoid. But really, he has good reason. With all those people gathered around the lake, somebody would have carried it back to the Safehaven for sure. Some of those guys are capable of doing anything. Anyway he's at work now."

Recovering from my astonishment enough to begin to think, I said, "Thanks for calling. You sort of caught me by surprise." I pushed a legal pad and pen in front of Sherry, hoping she would get the message and not say anything. I had the feeling Desiree would hang up if she knew there was more than one person listening. "We are sure there are people at the tavern who know more about the Finn's death than they are saying. Can you help us sort it out?"

This earned me a long silence. At my prodding she finally said she didn't know anything about it beyond what she had already told us. Resisting the urge to argue the point, I asked, "How about drugs at the tavern? We think the two might be connected. Who is the big pusher down there?"

This gained me some more silence. When I pushed she said, "You ask some big questions. Maybe Cleave is right. Maybe I should keep my mouth shut before somebody shuts it for me."

Sherry had scrawled, tell her we can subpoena her, but I was sure it would result in her hanging up. Instead, I apologized and assured her I wasn't about to tell anyone where I got my information. It still got me no answers. I was beginning to wonder why she called. I asked, "Who all works down there? We know about Younger and Melannie of course, and that other one, Helen, what's her name. Any one else?"

"Jefferies, Helen Jefferies is her name." At my grunt of acceptance she added, "There is Jerry Olsen. He opens up most mornings… Probably five-six days a week. He is a real alcoholic. Never lasts much beyond noon… Moves to the other side of the bar for a couple beers and he is totaled. Catches a cab home. They say he hasn't seen a sunset in ten years."

"He doesn't sound like a likely suspect. Nobody else?"

"There's Hazel. I don't even know her last name. She subs sometimes when people are sick or want a day off. Not very often. Only days as far as I know."

"That leaves us with three. We have it on good authority that the drug thing was around before Melannie came." Desiree began to agree and then caught herself. I glanced at the pad. Sherry had written, ask about customers. I said, "Now it's down to two. Unless of course it is a customer?" I let the question hang.

So did she. So I asked, "Any of the customers hanging around who don't work but always have lots of money to drink on."

"Half the guys in there don't work. They let some woman work to support them or find a woman who is on welfare. That's what I meant when I told you Cleave was good to me and went to work regular. Most of them are users and would be happy to get you a fix if they would be included, but I don't know any who are really pushing."

"That leaves us with two. Younger is a slug, not above it, but I don't think he has smarts enough to get away with it for as long as it has been going on." More silence. "On the other hand, little old Helen comes across as a nobody. Just a barmaid." Still no answer, so I asked if the silence meant she agreed or that she disagreed.

"It means that I think I have probably said too much already. I think I better go now."

I knew from the tone that arguing would probably get me nowhere, except maybe on her shit list. I spent a couple of minutes thanking her again for calling and suggesting she do so again if she heard anything new. Then I said, "Oh, There is one other thing…. You said this morning you talked to Riser and Hall. Did they say how long they had been waiting for us to come out?"

"I didn't talk to them. Cleave did. I got the impression they had been there quite a while and were getting tired of sitting."

I tried again, by asking if they mentioned who they were unhappy with for making them wait. I knew from the tone when she said, "I already told you I didn't talk to them," that the conversation was over, so I finished by telling her to give me a call if there was anything I could ever do to help her, trying to end on a friendly plane.

It earned me a zinger from Sherry. "Why didn't you tell her to call sometime when I wasn't here? Still think you got the hots for her. She didn't tell you anything. Why didn't you tell her we could subpoena her into court? Maybe that would get something out of her."

"She would have just hung up. Besides, she told us plenty."

"All I heard was silence when you asked your questions."

"Silence at the right time. When she didn't agree she spoke. You have to read between the lines."

"I can't take that into court."

"So we get something you can. Looks like we are left with Younger and Helen. I still can't see little Helen with enough juice to get all of those guys to defy the cops and do the things they have done. Even to killing people."

She said, "So that leaves Younger. I guess we need to investigate his finances. Follow the money. That's what they always say."

"But Melannie said he was about bankrupt."

"We both questioned her motives at the time."

We finally decided I should call Bernie and get what I could from him. I got Richardson instead. "Bernie is out on the highway. I'm not sure how long he will be. Something I can help you with?" I told him what we were up to and asked if he knew what sort of car Younger was driving. "Just a minute," he said, and I could hear him on the radio. He was laughing when he came back on the phone. He said, "Bernie questioned your intelligence, but said give you whatever it is you need."

"What sort of car does he drive?"

I could hear the click of computer keys and then, "Plymouth, four door, nineteen eighty nine." When I asked about lien holders in hopes of finding his bank, he answered, "Not anymore. He bought it used and has owned it for over five years."

"Doesn't sound like what a drug kingpin would be driving." At his acquiescence I asked if he knew where the man lived. Suggesting maybe he had invested his money in a big house instead.

"Car titles list street addresses." After another interval he was back with six twenty nine fifth. "That would be up on the hill by the middle school. On that road that goes around past the high school. In that area the house probably isn't much better than the car." When I thanked him for his help, he said, "I agree with Bernie, you should leave it to us. These guys have already been responsible for two deaths. I'd hate to see one of you get hurt."

"Me too. I wouldn't like that a bit." I thanked him for his help and cradled the phone.

Everything in Oceanside is close, the town is that small. We could have walked, but Sherry chose to drive the quarter mile. We found fifth easily enough, but almost none of the houses sported numbers. We drove all the way over the hill and found a number on the school, and then counted backwards. The only house it could be didn't say what we wanted to hear so we went down to the highway and worked our way back up from the other end of the street.

We ended up at the same place. A small two-bedroom shake house.

Probably built before 1950. It didn't look like it had been painted in almost that time. It also needed a roof and there were a couple of windows that must be out or cracked as they had plastic over them. There was a glassed in porch across the south side that undoubtedly had a nice view of the river once, but the shrubs like the lawn had not been trimmed in a long time and were grown up to where they usurped any possible view.

We sat and looked. Nobody said anything for several minutes. Finally Sherry said, "This has to be a mistake. That house goes with the old Plymouth. That's not the home of a man with money. It confirms what Melannie said. He doesn't have any money."

"We are some kind of detectives. We just eliminated our last suspect. Where do we go now?"

Sherry slowly turned around in a driveway and headed down the hill. We both counted houses again in hopes we could change what we knew was unchangeable. At the stop sign at the bottom of he hill we sat and waited for an opening to make a right turn onto the highway.

The second car to pass was a late model Buick station Wagon. Black, with all of its side windows also tinted black. Before it passed we both caught the flash of a white face through the windshield. A face that was turned quickly away from us, but not before we recognized the driver.

"That was what's her name?"

Sherry supplied, "Helen Jeffries. The little nobody. Hell of a nice car for someone earning minimum wages to be driving." Sherry allowed one more car to pass and then whipped out in front of the empty log truck that was following. His tires smoked as he stood on his brakes. I'll wager the blue smoke was just as thick inside the truck cab as outside, as he laid on his air horn to express his feelings.

I swallowed hard and said, "If she didn't know we were following her before she does now."

"What was I supposed to do? I couldn't just let her get away." I thought, *how could anyone get away when there is only one street available?* But I'm learning. I kept my mouth shut.

Two blocks down highway 101 turns right, but the Buick continued straight ahead. The car in between turned and we found ourselves right behind the black car. The Buick sped up and Sherry started to follow suit until I said, "Slow down, let her think she is getting away. See where she goes."

Two blocks down she turned left. On a road with only two possible destinations. It winds out to a lighthouse and park; both deserted this time of year, or to an exclusive residential area on a hillside, with posh houses looking out over the river to Astoria. Neither sounded too likely. The second didn't sound like a barmaid, but might very well go with the fancy car.

When Sherry turned the corner we discovered the Buick, almost stopped, about half a block down the road, obviously waiting to see if we were going to follow. When we turned the corner, she sped away. But not before I was able to get her license number. At the second cross street she braked suddenly then accelerated up the street to her left, leaving us the choice of obviously following or losing her.

By the time we reached the corner where she had turned, she was two blocks down and turning right without bothering to stop. Sherry started to follow suit until I pointed out the Buick was undoubtedly heading for the Safehaven Tavern. For once we agreed. Neither of us wanted another session like the last one at the tavern, and under the circumstances knew it would undoubtedly be much worse.

We sat and talked, but could come up with nothing more we could do. I suggested, since we had eaten nothing since morning and we were only half a block from the Bar View, maybe we could discus it over dinner. Sherry zinged me with, "You just want your ego stroked by that big tit blonde." But she pulled around the corner, did a quick U-turn, and parked across the street from the restaurant.

CHAPTER TWENTY-FOUR

Doris was watching TV while she filled catsup bottles. The place was devoid of customers. She gave me a big smile and a throaty, "Hi Tom." Sherry got only a nod, but I don't think she even noticed the slight. We headed through to a back table and the blonde picked up a pair of menus and the coffee pot and followed. She poured the coffee, but didn't offer the menus. I suspect they never change and most of her regulars order from memory.

I threw her a curve by saying, "Give us a few minutes," and removed the menus from under her arm. She moved away without comment, which was comment enough. I began scanning my copy and asked, "What do you think?"

"How can you think of eating? She has to be the one." Her quick change of direction caught me still thinking food. At my questioning look she added, "Helen. The simple little barmaid. She has been there all of the time, invisible, but there."

"But we have no proof."

"Proof hell. She's probably over at the tavern stirring up her troops. They tried to kill us once today already, and that was before we saw

179

her in her fancy car. She damn sure won't let it slide if she is the one."

"I agree, we need to check her out, but it's almost too late to do it today and we are going into the weekend." Hard to believe it had only been a week. We can call Bernie, but that would just confirm she owns the Buick and far as I'm concerned, that was rather obvious."

"We need to do something or it's going to be a long two days. I'm scared. We can't keep being as lucky as we were this afternoon."

Pointing out that the truck thing happened before noon wouldn't have gained me any points, so I said, "We are here, so let's eat, and then try to find Bernie. I know he doesn't have enough men to watch us all of the time, but maybe he can have them hang around enough to spook the drunks." I signaled Doris and when she came over I asked her to bring us two fish and chip dinners. Sherry wrinkled her nose but made no comment. She really must have been worried.

We talked while I ate and she picked at her food. Trying to fit Helen into what we knew and what had happened. I finally suggested we should go back to my place and dig up the computer file of what we knew and see if we could figure out where she was when things happened. See if we could make it fit her. Sherry said, "I thought all those files were erased." I told her about the copies I had run earlier and stuffed in the book.

We were interrupted by the arrival of four guys. Rather loud guys. Obviously they had been drinking, and it took little imagination to figure where. They sat down at a table about half way between us and the door, and their interest in us was obvious. Sherry shriveled in her chair. I didn't feel much braver. I expected them to try to create an argument that would get us involved. They sat and talked in loud voices and looked our way frequently, but made no overt moves.

I decided it was to be a war of nerves. They had been sent to keep an eye on us and to worry us, but not to attack. At least not here in front of a witness. I pointed this out to Sherry and she said, "It is damn well working. I'm scared. Let's get the hell out of here."

"I think that's what they want. Out there it's getting very dark and we would be alone." I didn't mention the others who might be waiting also. "Wait a few minutes and I'll go and call Bernie. See if he has a car in the area."

After a visit from Doris the guys quieted down some. It was only too obvious. All four ordered just coffee and none were in any hurry to drink it. The quieting seemed to ease Sherry's mind some. She began to relax, part way. Until I told her I had an idea and outlined it for her. I would try to run a bluff with a call to the cops. When I started to get up, she said, "You're not going to leave me here."

"I need you here. I want them to know I'm going to come back. The phone is up there by the door and I'm afraid they will think we are leaving if we both go." Her expression said she wasn't sure, but she sank back on her chair. I then made a show of checking my change and asked her if she had a quarter for the phone, just to be sure they were watching.

At the phone, I dropped in a quarter and punched in the number of the cop shop. I turned toward Sherry as I waited, which was just incidentally toward the foursome, so I could be sure they would hear who I was talking to. Richardson answered. In a voice loud enough for the others to hear I called him by name, told him who I was, and asked to speak to Bernie. I was sure the town was small enough and they had been in enough contact with the law that all four knew who I was talking to. I turned back to the phone while he explained that the hospital had called to let them know that Riser was showing signs of coming around so Bernie was back there waiting to talk to him. I thanked him and told him quietly, I would try to call Bernie at the hospital.

When he hung up I stood and carried on an imaginary conversation with the dead phone, occasionally turning to look at the guys, and speaking loud enough for them to catch the words I wanted them to hear. I finally thanked Bernie and hung up the phone that was saying for about the fifth time, "If you want to make a call, hang up and dial again," in its metallic feminine voice.

On the way back to our table I gave the four at the other table, by now a much quieter foursome, a knowing smile. Sherry met me with, "Is Bernie going to come down and rescue us again?"

Her shoulders sagged when I told her he was at the hospital and wouldn't be arriving. She brightened somewhat when I explained that the guys didn't know he wasn't coming and told her what I had in mind. "We will sit here and watch the street as if we expect him. The first car goes by slowly we will act relieved and get up and go out to the car and go see Bernie. It's dark enough that with any luck they won't be able to tell it's not a police car and it's only about four blocks to the hospital."

I motioned Dorothy over on the pretext of filling our cups, and paid her for the fish. We sat and watched for what felt like hours and no cars came by. Sherry was beginning to get agitated and I was beginning to wonder about my planning. Finally a car went by and Sherry started to get to her feet. I shook my head no and said, "It was going too fast and in the wrong direction, probably heading for the Safehaven. We want them to think it will be waiting for us down the block."

"But we could sit here all night before we get a slow car, heading in the right direction."

We sat for at least another ten minutes, and I was beginning to think her right, when a car came from the other direction. It went by slowly and I caught the restaurant lights reflecting off the faces of the occupants. I suspect it was the same car as before. It had probably been to the tavern, and the people in it had heard about the standoff at the Barview and they were driving by slowly because they were curious about what was going on inside.

I took her by the arm and said, "That's our cue. Let's do it," hoping the others had not seen as much as I because they might have recognized the car. I was afraid Sherry was going to break into a run. As we passed the other table I managed another grin and hoped it didn't look quite as sick on the outside as it felt from the inside.

Outside in the car, I said, "Pull a quick U-turn and head for the hospital, they probably won't be expecting that. I think this is definitely a good night to spend with Bernie." Looking back over her shoulder I could see two faces at the window and another man was standing in the doorway, but no one was hurrying out to follow us. They probably hadn't thought far enough ahead to have brought a car. As we went past the Gull there was a four-wheeler sitting across the street. It was all dark so I couldn't tell if someone was sitting inside watching for our return or if it was just parked there. I no longer trusted coincidences.

At the hospital we parked alongside the police car in the all but vacant lot and hurried to the nearby entrance. I shouldered the door with one arm and urged Sherry in with the other, but the damn thing was locked. I rattled the door and peered in to the dimly lighted lobby. There was nobody in sight, and the place felt deserted. Sherry finally found a small sign saying, "This door is locked after six p.m. Go to emergency entrance at the north end of the building." An arrow pointed off to the left.

I backed up and looked to the left. The building looked a mile long, with shrubbery all the way, and the lot was dimly lighted. Feeling rather exposed, I led Sherry to the corner. The north side of the building was even darker. The only light came from a blue and white sign reading, 'Ambulance Entrance'. Hand in hand we made a run for it across the lawn. This door didn't open either. I could see a woman at a desk inside, but she paid us no attention. I spotted a bell along side the door with a sign reading, ring for service.

I stabbed it with my thumb and the woman inside looked up with an annoyed expression. She leaned toward a box on her desk and in a tired voice she asked, "Can I help you?" She didn't sound as if she really was interested in being of help, only in getting rid of us.

"We need to get inside."

"What do you want?"

My back was feeling more and more exposed. I said, "We need to talk to Bernie."

"Who is Bernie? Visiting hours isn't till eight. You'll have to come back."

I tried to explain, but she went back to whatever she had been doing and was obviously going to ignore me. I leaned on the button and could hear the bell ring through the door. After a few seconds she said, "Go away, or I will call security."

I said, "Please do." I figured security would probably know if the police were in the building. It obviously wasn't what she expected to hear, but she still didn't move. I punched the button again and held it down. She didn't react for a while, but eventually picked up the phone. A man in green finally appeared and spoke briefly with her and then came over and opened the door. He didn't look any too friendly, but he did listen.

I guess he figured we couldn't be too bad if we wanted to chat with the cops. He indicated we should follow and crossed the room where he opened a second door with a key on a chain he produced magically from under his shirttail. When he was finished with it he let go and it vanished again. One of those retractable gadgets that clip on the belt, but entirely hidden by his green shirttail. I was just happy there were two doors locked between us and anyone who might be looking for us.

He had me totally lost before we rounded a final corner and there was Bernie, slumping in a hospital chair that appeared two sizes too small and very uncomfortable. He had a Styrofoam cup dangling from his big paw. He appeared to be asleep, but when we approached, he surprised me with, "Evening Ankus, looking for another story?"

"Told you we would let you know if we stumbled onto anything."

"And I told you if you had any smarts you would leave the stumbling to us."

"But we saw Helen Jefferies this afternoon in her fancy station wagon."

"That yellow Toyota?"

"Buick. Fancy new black Buick."

"She drives a rusty old yellow Toyota station wagon. I've checked it out before."

"She also drives a brand new, black Buick station wagon." At his dubious expression I produced the scrap of paper with the license number and explained how we got it.

He studied it momentarily and then heaved up out of the chair. The groans attested to the length of time he had been sitting there. He crossed to the nurses' station and asked to use a phone. "John… Run me a license number." After a pause he started writing on my paper.

I read over his shoulder. 2002 Buick… Wagon… Registered owner, Helen Jefferies…. Remembering his check of the previous day I asked, "Where did she finance it?"

He asked the question of the phone, and said, "No shit." Then covered the phone and said, "No lien holder. She must have paid cash."

When I asked where she bought it he asked and then said, "Origin is Oregon. Could have been Astoria, or it could have been Portland."

"What's it worth? Twenty-five thousand?"

"Probably about." He then asked John for the registered address and whistled through his teeth, "Geeze, expensive neighborhood for a barmaid." We were interrupted by the nurse, who said Riser was waking up. He told Robinson to round up some help, without putting too much on the air and that he would get back to him. All of us went two doors down the hall and entered a room.

The room was small and Bernie's large frame and the hovering nurse took up most of it. Sherry and I stood in the doorway. I expected to find the man totally swathed in bandages, but all that was visible were a couple of band-aid size plasters on one side of his face. Bernie was talking in a low voice and I could only hear bits and pieces. Riser wasn't buying it, from the sullen expression on his face. He finally said, "You can't prove anything."

Bernie straightened up and snapped out, "You can't deny you were driving your truck this morning. We have several witnesses to that. Driving it in a very reckless manner. Gordon Riser, I am placing you under arrest for the murder of Karl Hall." At Riser's look of disbelief, he added, "He didn't make it." He proceeded to read the man his rights.

No, "I feel bad about Hall," or "I'm sorry he is dead," Riser just said, "I want a lawyer."

"You will be able to call one. I hope you aren't counting on Helen Jefferies to get you one. She has a mess of trouble of her own. We picked her up with a load of drugs. We were talking to her when they called me down here to talk to you. She is claiming she is just a user and that you are the big supplier. The stuff she was hauling was for you."

"That's a lot of bullshit."

"What? That she said it or that you are dealing?"

"I ain't saying any more. I want to talk to a lawyer."

"OK. We are waiting right now for a warrant. We are going to take your house apart. If we find any drugs I will be back to charge you with that one too."

"You can't do that with me laying here in the hospital. I want to talk to my lawyer."

"Oh yes we can. With her statement that you are her pusher, any Judge in the county would give us a warrant. When you talk to your lawyer, ask him if we can do it."

"I'm not the supplier. Helen is the supplier. Her and her fancy car and her fancy house and her fancy friends from Portland. She has been supplying half the peninsula for years. She got Younger hung up on the stuff so she could con him into giving her a job at the tavern. She just works there so she can peddle the stuff."

Bernie flashed us a triumphant grin and said, "Thanks. That's all I need. I agree, you better talk to an attorney." He walked back out to the nurses' station and pointed at the phone. When the nurse nodded, he picked it up and dialed. "John, roust out a Judge and get us a warrant. Harriman is probably easiest. Yeah, Helen Jefferies. The address on the Buick registration. Drugs, and you better make it anything pertaining to the Finn's murder." He spent another five minutes recounting what had happened and giving instructions as to what to tell the judge, for a warrant covering controlled substance, as well as evidence relating to the murder of the Finn. He finished with, "We'll wait here to make sure nobody gets to Riser. Oh, and see if the county's drug dog is available."

It was over an hour before the cars began to arrive. Bernie parked them all behind the clinic, across the street. Both precautions proved to be fortunate as two of the Safehaven crowd showed for visiting hours. Bernie stationed one of the reserves in the door of Riser's room to observe their visit. With him there, they didn't say much, nor did they stay long.

It was almost two hours before the dog arrived and they were ready to move out. I spent most of the time thinking up a good argument as to why we should be allowed to attend the party. When it was time to go Bernie told them where we were going and to park away from the house, and not where they would be obvious. Approach would be on foot. When I finally broached the idea of our going, he looked at me for a minute, shook his head, and said, "Why not, I haven't been able to keep you out of it before. At least you will have about all of the protection available in the county, and I guess you have helped a little bit."

Bernie led off and we fell in behind. Next came another Long Beach car, and two County cars. Richardson brought up the rear. We snaked out the winding road toward the point, then turned up a steep hill where the houses were large and each on an oversize lot, looking out over the river toward Astoria. It was early enough that most houses still had their lights on, but streetlights were scarce.

Bernie stopped at a cross street and told the rest of us to park here. He would leave his car up beyond the house and walk back down. The street chosen for parking turned out to be a cul-de-sac and we made the loop and parked back at the entrance. The others lined up behind.

There was one man in each of the two county cars. I recognized Malahovsky even in the dark. The other was holding the leash of a large German Shepherd. There was one officer and one reserve in each of the city cars. Richardson immediately dispatched the two reserves and the other officer to the three houses on the street to inform the residents who we were and to tell them they should stay inside.

Bernie was back with the news that the house was dark, and he was betting vacant. He told two of the officers to try to get down to the back of the house, but to be careful because the lot was steep. We gave them a few minutes and then the rest of us trooped up the front walk and on to the porch. Bernie banged on the door, got no answer, and tried the knob. No luck. The place had that vacant feel.

Malahovsky asked, "Want me to open it?" And appeared disappointed when Bernie opted to try to find an easy way in. There was a garage to the right and the porch became a deck to the left. We followed it around and found it continued all across the front of the house. The view was magnificent. The harbor, including the Safehaven, in the foreground, with the river and the boat harbor behind. Off in the distance the lights of Astoria were dimly visible through the haze.

The sliding glass door was not even locked. We crowded inside.

Someone found a light switch and with the click we found ourselves in a very nice living room. The lady had taste. I noticed all of the men had on rubber gloves. Richardson saw we didn't and pulled out two pairs and offered them to Sherry and me.

We waited while the man with the dog made the tour of the house. There was no reaction until they reached the back end of the hallway leading off the entry toward the garage. The dog wanted through that door.

The deputy opened the door slightly and fumbled the wall until he found the lights. The dog pulled him in and there it was. She had been getting away with it so long she wasn't even trying to conceal it. Right out in the open on the bench. Several white bags, balance scales, small plastic bags like resealable sandwich bags, and a cardboard box with plastic bags of pot.

I knew I was looking at tomorrow's headlines, but cursed because I was again without a camera. That problem was solved at least partly when the flashes began going off. Maybe I could talk Bernie out of some of their pictures.

Bernie kept poking around while the others cataloged the drugs. I turned at his satisfied grunt and found him peering into a brown paper sack. He held it out for me to look inside. It contained a quart bottle of rubbing alcohol and two hypodermic syringes. He said, "It wasn't even hidden. Just stuffed into a corner. That broad didn't think we had smarts enough to ever turn her."

We all milled around complimenting each other on the good job for a while. Sherry hadn't said a dozen words since we left the restaurant. She finally said, "I'm beat. How about we head back to the Gull before someone gets hurt." At my questioning look she said, "Somebody is going to throw a shoulder out of joint or something, trying to pat himself on the back." I'm not sure all of the laughter was for real.

Bernie reminded us that Helen was still on the loose and promised to have a car check on us later so we stumbled down the hill through the darkness to her car. Five minutes later we pulled into the Gull parking lot. She asked the question that was getting to be an undesirable habit. "Did we leave the lights on when we left?"

"I don't remember. It was daylight so maybe we just didn't notice."
I was reasonably sure we hadn't left them on, but people prowling my
stuff was no longer new. Pissed me off, but you can get used to most
anything.

I suggested she wait while I did a quick check of the place, but
Sherry didn't want to stay outside in the dark, even though there were
no other cars in sight. We pushed open the door and entered, blinking
in the light.

It was like the story of the three bears. Not only had someone been
in my place, but she was still there. She said, "Come on in, Leave the
door open." She was looking over the top of what looked like a toy
pistol. Probably a nickel-plated thirty-two, but the hole that was pointed
our way looked more like a forty-five. I heard a noise behind me and
turned to see two of the local goons push in behind us and shut the
door.

CHAPTER TWENTY-FIVE

Sherry screamed and backed into me. I would have backed up myself, but there was about five hundred pounds of beef behind me. Helen Jefferies, little Helen the bit player, calmly looked over the nickel-plated automatic in her hand and said, "Come on in and sit down. Over there on the bed."

I figured this would be the place where the two goons would tie us up. That's how it always works in the movies. I guess she didn't think we were worth it. They continued to stand in front of the door, which was just as effective. Nobody said anything further.

It was eerie. The silence went on forever. It was probably only ten minutes, but I'm sure I aged at least five years. By the grip Sherry had on my arm, I knew she was at least as scared. I finally rose up and asked, "What are we sitting here waiting for?" Actually, I wasn't sure I wanted to know. Under the circumstance, I couldn't think of any answer that might be good.

Helen didn't bother to answer beyond waving her shiny little pistol our way. I was willing to accept that answer. I sat back on the bed, but I damn sure didn't relax.

After another long interval of silence, one of the goons asked, "How long we going to have to wait?"

"Until they get here." Helen turned toward us and added, "I've got friends coming. From out of town. They want to meet you." Her voice hardened and I could see the white lines around her mouth. She was losing her cool. She added, "You were warned several times, but you wouldn't listen. Had to keep messing around in things that weren't your business. When you saw me coming back from Portland in the Buick today I knew. I knew something had to be done with you so I called them."

She didn't explain what she knew, or who the "them" were, but I got the message. I said, "I don't understand. We were just trying to find out who killed the Finn. We knew that the Beasley kid didn't do it." I saw it was the wrong thing to say and shut up.

She jumped out of her chair with fire in her eyes. Pistol waving in my face she screamed, "You God damned fool. You have ruined everything. You cost my friends a lot of money. You can bet they didn't drive all the way down here from Portland to forgive and forget. This is the second trip they have made because of you," which I figured explained the computer thing. She pulled herself together with an effort and returned to her chair where she sat and panted as if she had just run a four-minute mile.

The two goons stood leaning against the doorframe and the rest of us sat. She slowly relaxed, but apparently only on the outside. It was probably only another five minutes until she picked up her purse, laid the gun on the table, and fished a cell phone out of the bag. She punched in a number that she obviously knew by heart. She grew more agitated as she listened to what had to be several rings at the other end. She started to drop the phone from her ear when her eyes lit and she snapped it back to her head. In a deferential tone she said, "I am just wondering how long before you get here." After a pause, "Okay. We have them here at his room at the Blue Gull. We will hold them until you get here."

I'm not sure where I got the nerve, but I finally asked, "I still don't understand. I'm sure you know we have most of it figured out, but we still don't know why."

Her color started to come up again, but at least she didn't pick up the gun. She asked, "You got what figured out? Just what the hell do you think happened?"

I wanted to say, "We know you killed the Finn, and we know you were responsible for the threats to us," but I thought better of it. I thought briefly of telling her about the raid on her house. And rejected that one too. I finally said, "The autopsy report showed the Finn was killed by a poison injection. The police think you were responsible. Nobody can figure how you would benefit from it."

"That goddamn big tit blonde…. It's all her fault. She had to come along and mess it all up."

I almost, but not quite had to laugh. Those were the same words Sherry used to describe the gal at the Bay View Café. I said instead, "Mess what up? I don't get it."

She stood up and began pacing. The gun was still on the table, but way out of my reach. "It doesn't make any difference. You aren't going to be able to tell anybody anyway. Everything was going perfect. I had Younger strung out on coke. I even had to sleep with that slimy son of a bitch a couple of times to get him there. After I got him hooked I was running the joint but he was getting the credit. It was going so smooth. He was using so much I even had to put a few bucks back into the tavern to keep him from going broke. Then that blonde showed up and he went all silly over her. She was so stupid. She would do anything he wanted, including sleeping with him, and all she wanted was to work in that crumby joint."

"I still don't understand what you…"

She cut me off with, "Jesus you are dense. Drugs. I had the whole damn peninsula. If the cops ever got onto it they would think it was Jack. Nobody ever noticed me."

She was right there; we totally discounted her as a suspect. The cops did also. I asked, "But why kill the Finn?"

"The cops were supposed to blame Melannie. Get her out of my hair for good. They had loaded him with so much straight alcohol he was blind. I figured a little more would do him in. I didn't think they would be able to tell the difference. It was easy; they were loading him into the cab. Nobody was noticing me. I slipped out and went by the drug store and got a quart of alcohol. I always have needles in the car. I followed him home and waited until I thought he was passed out."

"What about the maul that was leaning against the bed?"

"It was on the porch. I took it with me, just in case he came to or something. I knew he wouldn't appreciate it if he came to and found me giving him the needle. Afterwards, I poured some alcohol on a shirt lying on the bed and wiped it down. I still don't understand how they could tell the difference in the alcohol."

"If you had made him drink it they might not have. But in the vein it showed up because there was no chemical change like what would happen in the stomach or some such thing." She noticed me eying the gun on the table. She didn't pick it up, but she did move over next to the table and then sat down. I added, "You should look it up in a poison book. That's some nasty shit you laid on that poor fisherman. Hell of a way to die."

"Stupid fisherman. Younger and that blonde bitch would have done him in sooner or later anyway. Then with her insurance money he wouldn't need me at all. I had to get her blamed. With no money he would have crawled back on his hands and knees. I didn't want that dumb kid blamed. He walked in at the wrong time and screwed it all up."

"That's all we were doing. We knew Jimmy didn't kill him. But the county attorney wouldn't let it go. Figured he had a winner. Only way we could get the kid off was to find someone else. How were you able to sic all of the goons on us?"

"That was easy. They are a bunch of losers. A few free samples and they'll do anything." The goons at the door didn't look too pleased with this, but neither said a word.

Headlights washed across the windows. One of them moved over and peered out through the steamed up glass. "Big white sedan."

"That's them. Sorry, but I guess our pleasant little chat is over. Open the door for them," as she moved toward it with a smile.

The smile faded quickly. As the door was pulled open, it framed Bernie and John Robinson. Each had a gun held casually in his hand.

Beautiful big guns. Bernie said, "Evening Miss Jefferies… Ankus… Counselor… Seems I should know you two, but I can't remember the names at present, but I'm sure I will after tonight. Mind if we come in?" As they stepped forward the parking lot suddenly filled with red and blue flashing lights. The bulky figure of Sergeant Malahovsky filled the doorway. He didn't say anything…. The wide grin said it all.

We watched as the white-faced woman and her muscle were cuffed and read their rights. The cute little gun was still on the table. As Robinson was leading her toward the door she said, "I don't understand. How did you know we were here? How did you get their Lincoln?"

Bernie said with a smirk, "You invited us lady." He added, "We raided your place tonight. You're real busted." He turned to me and explained, "After you left her place, I left them to do an inventory. I went to get my car from where I parked it up the hill. I came back down the hill just as the white Lincoln pulled into the driveway. I warned the guys with the radio and pulled in behind him and hit my flashers. They were visiting a known drug house so we hooked them up and shook them down. They were all packing and no permits. When we impound a car we have to inventory the contents. You know… Make sure we don't lose any of their property. Seemed to make them awful nervous, so we decided to wait until we had a warrant. Just in case they show up in court with a smart lawyer," with a wink at Sherry.

"Anyway, while we were waiting for a tow to get there, the car phone rang. I never could ignore a ringing phone." Turning to Helen, he added, "It was you calling. And you invited us down."

Sherry found her voice, sort of. "Bernie. Are we glad…? Guess we owe you another thanks. Seems you are always rescuing us."

"I think I suggested a time or two that you should stay out of it. You could have got hurt."

"Everyone wanted us to stay out… Especially her," with a gesture at Helen. "I had to protect my client. It didn't look like anybody else was apt to figure it out."

"We usually get there eventually. Have to admit you may have speeded us up a bit. Course it really wasn't my case to worry about." He turned to Malahovsky and repeated it. "It's not my case. Guess that means you get to take them north. You also get to do all the paper work. You can have all the glory. Me, I'm going home to bed."

We watched as the three were led off and the police cars vanished, one by one. I closed the door and turned. Sherry wrapped me up in her arms. I held her as she went from shivering to quiet and I thought it was over. Then I became aware of the wetness on my chest. She was crying quietly. Meaning to comfort, I wiped her face with my handkerchief and said, "It's all over now. They won't be coming back. We won't have to worry about somebody busting down the door any more."

"Damn fool. Can't you tell when I am happy?"

Women's logic. Sometimes it escapes me. After a suitable interval I steered her to the bed. Some cuddling and she relaxed so I began to explore. I got no real objections until she murmured, "That's all you ever think of."

I couldn't let it pass. "That's because that is all I ever get... To think about it." It was some time later, when this was no longer true. We were both half asleep when it hit me. I raised myself up and asked, "Where did you ever learn to drive like that?" At her baffled look, "Up there by the lake this morning? Surprise me. You saved our hides."

"I grew up on *Starsky and Hutch* and *The Dukes of Hazard*. That's how they always did it."

Saved by a damn TV rerun. Like I said, I'll never understand women's logic.

Preview of the author's next book follows:

INVITATION TO MURDER

CHAPTER I

It was one of those days. One of those January days when the weather was so lousy I should have been happy I was able to sit in front of my computer instead of having to be out in it. One of those days the locals cite as what makes the beach livable. Weather so bad it keeps the tourists, lovably referred to as the pukers by the natives, away from the beach for over half of the year.

It still hadn't been bad enough to motivate me to accomplish anything toward the great American novel I have been attempting. My name is Tom Hill, and I like to call myself a freelance writer, though it's been more free than writer since I got lucky with my first book a few years ago. Between the skimpy royalties and an occasional stringer fee from the newspaper across the Columbia River, I am able to live in this paradise, billed by the local chamber of commerce as, "God's Best Effort." So long as I don't expect to eat too regular, and am not too proud about where I live.

Actually I live in the Blue Gull, a long time retired motel in Ocean Side, Washington. The motel has a lot of water-stained walls, more than its share of mildew, high heat costs because it has no insulation and broken down furniture including a sagging bed. Its one redeeming feature is that the rent is cheap.

The town has one traffic light, one convenience store, one service station, one restaurant, and four taverns or bars. The bus that runs through once in awhile has a sign on its rear stating, "Pacific County, God's Best Effort."

The door swung open and my other reason for staying in this supposed paradise blew in with a shower of rain. Sherry Thompkins… Auburn hair… Green eyes… No Twiggy, but every pound is a plus. I picture the bus sign plastered across her behind. During the week she is an attorney and I've never been able to figure out how I got so lucky. She slums by spending most weekends with me.

She opened with, "Don't just sit there and gape. Get off your butt and take some of this stuff so I can get this dumb door closed before we drown. God it's wet out there."

"What'd you do, pick up your cleaning?" Usually she leaves her stuff that needs cleaning, meaning her lawyer clothes, at her own pad. We are less formal here. The less the better, both formal and clothes, is my first choice.

"No… I went across the river and picked up your tux."

"My tux? I don't own any tux."

"You don't ever listen to me. It's a rental I reserved for you about ten days ago. It's a damn good thing I remembered because the store isn't open tomorrow and you'll have to have it tomorrow night."

I didn't have a clue. I knew I was on thin ice, but I said, "Why would I need a tux? I don't even go places where I need a tie if I can help it." As I stood there holding the stupid thing, trying to remember what she was talking about, without asking, because I knew I was probably in trouble and wasn't interested in digging myself into a hole I would just have to climb out of to have any sort of friendly evening ahead.

I could see I was getting in deeper. She said, "I told you at least two weeks ago we were invited to the murder." When I still drew a blank she added, "I told you they had invited us to the museum for their annual mystery dinner... Because we helped to solve the murder of the Finn Fisherman.... Damn, you never listen to me."

Like I said, I don't know how I got so lucky. Still drawing a blank, but looking for a way out, I said, "Oh... Was that this weekend?" as I hung the dripping garment bag in the small curtained off area that passes as a closet. Then I made my next mistake. I added, "Maybe I should call Charley and see if he needs it for his front page."

I knew I was wrong again when she came back with, "That's all you ever think of! A chance to sell a story to that damn paper. I thought it would be nice to dress up and rub elbows with some of the local big shots. Besides, maybe some of them will remember me when they need a lawyer."

I saw the trap in time, before I pointed out the similarity of our positions, and asked, "That was Saturday night? Tomorrow night? You going to wear one of those dresses where you need the double sticky tape?" Just picturing it made me warm.

She ignored my words and asked, "Got any coffee? I'm cold." She walked by the thermostat and cranked it up to the top. She knows that bugs me, but I knew better than to say anything.

"It's been coffee a long time. I'll put on a new pot... Only take a few minutes. Maybe we can work on warming you up while we wait." The expression on her face told me to drop it, so while the coffee cooked I dug through the sink and found two mugs and washed out yesterday's dregs.

"We never did get up to Dennis Company and buy you some dishes."

This is a revival of a past conversation that I have tried to forget also. My theory is, if you don't have many dishes, you never have a big stack to wash. I moved over and wiped the steam off the window with the corner of the faded curtain and looked out at the rain swept parking lot, while I slipped the thermostat down to somewhere near seventy degrees with my hidden hand. Nothing was moving on the street. Even the seagulls had moved inland to find better weather.

I watched as a jacked up four-wheel drive pickup swished down the street and remembered a few weeks back when we had some less than pleasant experiences with them. I followed its taillights until it had passed the Bay View Café curved around toward the docks. Probably heading for either the fish cannery or the Safehaven Tavern.